Kimberley Kill

Books by Barry Smith

The Kimberley Trilogy
For Freedom's Cause
Battle for the North
Kimberley Kill

Kimberley Kill

Barry Smith

Kimberley Kill

Published by Barry Smith

First published 2013
This edition published 2016

This is a work of fiction set in the near future and
all the characters and situations described are creations
of the author's imagination.

A Cataloguing-in-Publication record is available from
the National Library of Australia.

ISBN:
978 0 9953637 0 0 (pbk)
978 0 9953637 1 7 (ebk)

www.faceboook.com/BarrySmithWordSpinner

Dedication

My writings have been influenced by the following authors

DH Lawrence – whose Australian novel, *The boy in the bush,* first drew my attention to the Kimberley region.

Erskine Childers – who in his *Riddle of the sands* alerted British readers to the threat of potential invasion by Germany, before the outbreak of the First World War.

Neville Shute and Arthur Upfield – writers of English origin who, like me, transplanted themselves into Australian soil and grew to be ardent lovers of Australia and its bush.

Acknowledgements

My grateful thanks to

Jennifer for her skilful crafting of my
publicity materials and for the quilt that
draws customers to my market stalls.

Coral and Jill for challenging comments
and insightful suggestions.

Paul for all his advice and encouragement
and his team for pulling it all together.

Sandra – My dearest friend.
For always believing in me and urging me on.

Historical Note

The Nackaroos

The 2/1st North Australia Observer Unit (also known as the 'Nackaroos' and 'Curtin's Cowboys') was formed in 1942 as part of the defence of northern Australia from the Japanese during the Second World War, performing reconnaissance, scouting and coastal surveillance tasks across the Kimberley and the Northern Territory's sea and air approaches. As the Japanese threat subsided, patrols were reduced in July 1943, and the unit was disbanded in 1945.

Norforce

In 1981 the first Regional Force Surveillance Unit (RFSU), the North West Mobile Force (NORFORCE), was officially raised to meet the requirements for surveillance and reconnaissance in the north and north-west of Australia.

In 1985, two other RFSUs were raised: the Pilbara Regiment in Western Australia, and the 51st Battalion Far North Queensland Regiment in Cape York.

NORFORCE traces its history back to the formation of the 2/1 North Australia Observer Unit (2/1 NAOU) in1942.

NORFORCE is a unique organisation for many reasons. It has the largest area of operations of any military unit in the world today and is permanently assigned to a Joint Commander for ongoing surveillance operations in northern Australia. The unit relies heavily on the commitment and local knowledge of the population of northern Australia to fulfil its role. It has a high proportion of Aboriginal soldiers whose talents are fully utilised and remains well-equipped to undertake its tasks, whether Australia is at peace or at war.

Kopassus

Kopassus (Kommando Pasukan Khusus – Special Forces Command) is an Indonesian Army special forces group that conducts special operations missions for the Indonesian government, such as direct action, unconventional warfare, sabotage, counter-insurgency, counter-terrorism, and intelligence gathering.

Kopassus was founded on April 16, 1952. They made their mark by spearheading some of the government's military campaigns: putting down regional rebellions in the late 1950s, the Western New Guinea campaign in 1961–1962, the confrontation with Malaysia from 1962–1966, the massacre of alleged communists in 1965, the East Timor invasion in 1975, and the subsequent campaigns against separatists throughout Indonesia.

The unit saw action during the Indonesia-Malaysia Confrontation when in 1965, Indonesia launched a war for control of North Borneo (Sabah/Sarawak) during Malaysian independence, particularly in the Battle of Sungei Koemba. They were involved in clashes with British and Australian Special Forces and have gained an unsavoury reputation for ruthlessness in suppressing internal resistance outbreaks.

During times of favourable Australia-Indonesia relations, Kopassus units have trained with the Australian SAS.

The Kimberley

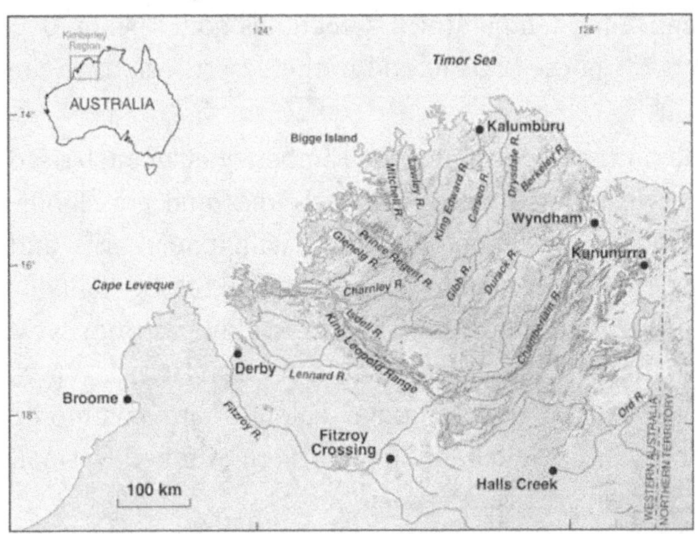

Geography

The Kimberley region extends from the dry red sand dunes of the Great Sandy Desert in the south through rugged sandstone escarpments of the sub-humid Kimberley Plateau and Timor Sea in the north. It extends east to the Northern Territory border. Covering some 423,500 square kilometres it is nearly twice the size of the State of Victoria and three times the size of England. Numerous islands off the northern coast and the many gulfs, headlands and the irregularity of the coastline attest to the current historically high sea levels and the so-called "drowned" topography of the region. There are more than 2500 mapped islands between Yampi Sound and the mouth of the King Edward River. In a straight line it is approximately 400 km from Yampi Sound to the mouth of the King Edward River whereas it is nearly 1300 km around the actual coastline.

The region experiences a tropical monsoonal climate. The wet season extends from November to March and the dry season from April to October. Annual rainfall peaks at 1500 mm per annum in the north west part of the plateau and drops off to 350 mm per annum in the semi-arid south. Temperature ranges can be extreme with summer day time temperatures frequently exceeding 40°C and winter night time temperatures sometimes going below 0°C on the higher parts of the plateau and in the desert regions to the south.

Most of the northern portion of the Kimberley is characterised by savannah style vegetation with mature trees and grasslands. Rivers to the north are commonly lined with paperbarks and pandanus. The river patterns are commonly defined by joints or faults in the underlying sandstones and most flow north or west and commonly incise deep gorges within the sandstone. Where the rivers meet the ocean mangrove colonies are commonly developed. Throughout much of the northern Kimberley small patches of rain forest are preserved.

Aboriginal occupation of the Kimberley

A growing body of archaeological work indicates that Aborigines arrived in Australia at least 55,000 years ago and it is possible that one of the first places occupied, given its proximity to Timor and New Guinea was the Kimberley area. Sea levels were probably about 80 metres below current levels, however, it is obvious from paleo-bathymetric maps that the early arrivals involved the traversing of 200–400km of open water. It is obvious from the extensive and prolific rock art (both Gwion Gwion and Wandjina styles) that occurs throughout much of the Kimberley that significant numbers of Aborigines lived and travelled throughout the region for thousands of years.

European exploration of the Kimberley

There is some uncertainty as to exactly when the first European contact was made in the Kimberley but that contact was obviously made from the coast as European exploration of the globe and the search for new resources extended south. The thousands of years of uninterrupted Aboriginal occupation was quickly brought to a conclusion once the first explorers and settlers arrived.

Forrest 1879

In 1879 Alexander Forrest led a major exploratory party into the Kimberley from Beagle Bay. The intent was to penetrate to the northern extremities of the region and the party successfully crossed the Oscar Ranges but found the King Leopold Range too difficult for their horses. The party was eventually recovered from Walcott Inlet, retreated by sea to the Fitzroy River and then, skirting the Napier Range eventually headed east to meet up with the Overland Telegraph Line in the Northern Territory.

Enroute to the Telegraph Line he crossed both the Ord and Victoria Rivers and his favourable report on the pastoral potential of the land was the trigger for the establishment of the cattle industry in the Kimberley region.

Brockman 1901

The rapid development of the cattle industry in the southern and eastern Kimberley together with other developments in the region prompted the State Government to commission the Chief Inspector Surveyor, Frederick Slade Brockman, in March 1901 to complete the mapping of the Kimberley. Brockman's party comprising eight Europeans and two Aboriginal prisoners from Rottnest Island left Wyndham on April 2, 1901 with 70 horses and provisions for six months. Amongst the group was the Government Geologist, Andrew Gibb Maitland and Dr F M House, a naturalist and botanist. The party initially headed south, following the Chamberlain River before turning west and reaching the Walcott Inlet before heading north eventually reaching Napier Broome Bay close to the present town of Kalumburu.

Reaching the mouth of the Drysdale River they followed the river south before returning to Wyndham in November 1901. In total the expedition covered more than 2300 km in a little over six months and named a number of rivers and prominent hills and ranges. There were no injuries to any of the party and although only limited numbers of Aborigines were encountered good relationships were maintained with the indigenous inhabitants.

Kimberley Kill

Kimberley Kill is a work of futuristic fiction. None of the events have happened and the plot and characters are the product of my imagination. But I am sure that these defenders of the North would be more than able to rise to these imagined challenges to Australia's security, if they were to occur.

Barry Smith
Melbourne 2013

Contents

1

Hostilities Begin

Somewhere in Sinai

Major Elat rode at the head of his hover-tank column back across the Sinai wastes, passing the broken and blackened carcases of Egyptian, Iranian and Iraqi tanks and the shattered personnel carriers, surrounded by the remains of dead infantrymen and Hezbollah irregulars. Shaking his head in amazement and turning to his sergeant he shared his disbelief.

"I can't understand why they tried to attack us again in open battle, Gideon, especially when the civil war between Sunnis and Shia has barely finished. Beirut, Cairo and Damascus are almost totally destroyed and the Iranian government is on its knees, now that their educated youth has rebelled against the Mullahs and their peasant militias. Thank God our sabotage stopped them becoming nuclear armed. They were crazy to believe that the Russians would come to their aid, when they are up to their eyes in trouble in Siberia and they sure underestimated the resolve of the Americans to back us when the Middle Eastern war broke out."

His Sergeant nodded his agreement. "Yes Major. Especially since the yanks stopped relying on Arab oil, went nuclear at home and became self-sufficient in energy. It's no wonder the Chinese reacted aggressively when their Gulf energy supplies were cut off. All we can do now is secure Israel's survival and hope that the troubles in the east will be short-lived and that our side wins."

Midnight in Moscow

Longing for the end of his shift Lieutenant Grigor Ribokov stretched and yawned. It was midnight on Saturday in Moscow and in frustration at his detention he yelled out across the silent control room.

"Why am I here chained to my monitor when my friends will be drinking and dancing the night away at my favourite bar and stealing all the girls?"

Despite the chorus of groans and cat-calls that greeted his outburst, his comrades shared the same frustration. But fear of losing their plumb jobs kept these Russian Military Intelligence analysts glued to their screens, monitoring increasing reports of computer failures and the shut-down of dependent machinery and power plants in all major, Russian cities.

Initial reports of communication black-outs between Far-East Defence Command and military bases in Irkutsk, Khabarovsk, Vladivostok and border outposts along the Chinese frontier caused little alarm. They were dismissed as the usual malfunctions of ailing and outdated systems. But when news of major energy companies losing contact with their key oil and gas installations throughout Eastern Siberia flashed onto his screen, Grigor realised that this was far from usual and was alerted to the growing hubbub in the normally silent monitoring centre as other analysts gave voice to their alarm at incoming reports from critical locations, or the lack of them.

"I've lost contact with Far East Command in Vladivostok!"

"Military and Civilian air traffic controls have lost contact with aircraft. Hundreds of planes are flying blind across Russian airspace!"

"TV and radio transmissions have gone off the air, just like that!"

Most ominously, early warning radar coverage of Eastern Russia had gone down and furious callers from high command demanded to know what was happening. Grigor turned and called out to his nearest colleague.

"What do you make of this? Surely it can't be just system failure?"

Before his partner could reply, all the computer screens went blank, the air conditioning stopped working and lights went out both in the control room and all over Moscow.

Eastern Siberia

In the Chinese army command drone, General Xai looked triumphantly at the map of his advancing forces' progress unfolding on his communication tablet and called to his aide for a summary of progress so far.

"All is going to plan General. Our massive cyber-attack caught the Russians completely by surprise and paralysed all their communication and defence response systems. Their major cities are without power, water, public health and banking services and already, this has led to outbreaks of unchecked mob violence which the Police are unable to bring under control. Their government is isolated, their military is blind and they are totally unable to defend themselves."

"Good. What is the status of our forward units?"

"For some time, we have been infiltrating special-forces units into border cities and amongst the substantial Chinese workforce that the Russians have imported to undercut the cost of their own labour. As planned these teams have gone into action"

"Good, but what progress have they achieved?"

"They have secured airstrips for our military cargo drones to land our best shock troops, backed by armoured and mobile artillery units. Those advancing from Chita have already occupied Irkutsk and are moving to secure the oil and gas fields. Marines have gone ashore in Vladivostok and on Sakhalin Island without meeting significant resistance. Our aerial reconnaissance and fighter drones have established unchallenged air supremacy."

"How have the Japanese and South Koreans reacted?"

"Not at all!, our diplomats' assurances that our move on the East Siberian energy areas would not threaten their supplies and that we would maintain their pipeline connections, seem to have prevented a backlash. The unexpected strength of their cyber defences has denied us dominance over them but they are well aware that our satellite-guided missile systems threaten their major cities and military installations. The guarantee of a reunited Korea pacified Seoul and the promised return of the Southern Kuril Islands to Japanese sovereignty has delighted Tokyo. Their submarines and satellites have shadowed our Northern Fleet's passage towards the Russian coast, but there have been neither incidents nor challenges."

"This is excellent news Colonel. Ensure my electronic map is kept completely up to date and wake me when the East Siberian oil and gas installations and those on Sakhalin have been secured and are controlled by our engineers. It will then be my pleasure to report the success of our mission, to our masters in Beijing."

Berlin

The President of the European Republic looked down from her office in the Reichstag on the growing mob of angry Berliners struggling to break through a protective cordon of riot police. They were intent on venting their fury on those who had stolen their democratic rights, made them totally dependent on Russian energy supplies and so degraded Europe's military forces that it was incapable of defending itself, let alone projecting sufficient power to defend its vital economic interests.

In the background her cabinet ministers argued loudly about how to resolve the crisis but could not unite behind a singular response. Turning to the Minister for France she sighed and expressed her fears for the immediate future of their great experiment.

"Marcel, I find it hard to believe and impossible to accept

that Europe is once more in danger of collapse. Despite all we have achieved in uniting peacefully under one government, the Republic and our great cities especially my beloved Berlin, are beset by forces within and by enemies without."

"Mais oui! Madame President. The fates have not been kind, despite our best intentions. We have made mistakes and we must now face the consequences. We were wrong to rely more on our climate experts' mathematical models than hard science. We turned away from nuclear power and put all our reliance on unproven alternative energy sources. Now we are at the mercy of unscrupulous Russian oil and gas suppliers."

"Even so, why do people scream blindly for a return to the inefficient, divisive, nation-states which could not fund our cherished welfare systems and compete effectively with aggressive Asian economies?"

"I share your concern. But then, as a Frenchman, I regret our inability to back-up our interests with credible force and look back wistfully to the days when France could punch above its weight, as it did in Mali some years ago. It is true that our unification has prevented a repeat of historical conflicts between our two great countries, but it is hard to swallow the arrogance of the British Prime Minister, who never ceases to remind us of their independent deterrent capability and close military and economic ties with the energy-rich, United States, Canada and Australia."

"Alas, it is true that we are no longer a nation of Panzers and we are at the mercy of forces from the east which we are powerless to challenge. I fear that we must look across the Atlantic and the Channel, yet again, for our salvation. Let us hope we are better able to afford the price they will demand this time."

In the South China Sea

On the luxury liner's bridge Fred Hanbury drew his wife's attention to the twinkling chains of lights that marked the location of the Chinese battle fleet stationed off Hong Kong.

"Look Darling, there's the Chinese navy and they are about let fireworks off to mark the start of their new year."

His wife, Lorna, acknowledged Captain Gregson's welcome and told him how much they appreciated his generous invitation to view the celebration from this privileged vantage point.

"We will look forward to telling our grandchildren all about this highlight of our cruise when we return to England."

"It's a pleasure Mrs Hanbury." Captain Gregson assured her. "It's the least we could do to mark your golden wedding anniversary and from here the display should be quite a sight."

Then, before the steward could serve the drinks, spectacular flashes of light turned night into day and the roar of massive detonations echoed across the sea, deafening the cruise ship's passengers.

"My God!" The captain gasped. "Those ships are under attack" and as he spoke, burning warships exploded, began to break-up and sink. It certainly was an unforgettable sight and much more than just a memorable pyrotechnic display.

Washington

In the Pentagon war-room, America's military chiefs had assembled to brief the President on the outbreak of hostilities in Asia and turned their attention to the giant wall monitor bringing into focus his image, beamed from a secure bunker, far away in the west.

"Mr President. We can now confirm that Chinese forces have taken control of all Russia's far eastern energy assets. Because of China's superior cyber-warfare capability and their massive pre-emptive strike on military assets and civilian utilities, Russia is totally unable to defend itself and is committing what forces it can muster to cope with the social disorder in most of its major cities."

"Thank you General for that status report, but can you explain why we have not received a similar strike to disable our defence capability?"

"Their main strategy was to secure vital energy supplies in close geographical proximity and they made moves to deter us from making any attempt to block their incursion into Siberia. They probed our cyber-defences but the strategic investment your predecessor made from enhanced oil and gas revenues to beef-up our technological warfare capabilities, really paid off. The 'nerds' we drafted from Silicon Valley firms and our key universities, were more than a match for the People's Liberation Army cyber-forces and they backed off with singed tail feathers."

"I understand, Admiral, we have lost some assets and suffered disruption of our defence systems. What is the status of our naval defences?"

"That is correct sir. Our Pacific carrier battle fleet was taking up station off Okinawa to monitor Chinese, Japanese and South Korean naval deployments when Chinese submarines launched an unprovoked attack. One of our carriers was sunk and two air warfare destroyers were badly damaged before our response took out two Chinese nuclear subs, forcing them to break off the engagement?"

"General, why didn't the Chinese attack in greater force and what should we do now?"

"Sir, we believe that their attack was motivated by frustration at their inability to overwhelm our cyber-defences and was intended as a warning to keep out of the South China Sea. Their assault would have been far worse had we not ordered our military space station to arm its nuclear rockets targeted on Chinese cities and signal our readiness to launch. The revelation of this secret facility had the desired deterrent effect and their only response was to disable our chain of communication satellites and almost all of our terrestrial relay stations covering North and South East Asia. We recommend a limited, reprisal attack on Chinese surface ships stationed off Hong Kong to emphasise that we will not tolerate their belligerence and limit their area of operation to the seas off the Chinese and Russian mainlands."

"Are they meeting resistance from any other countries?"

"No other country has attacked them but they are wary of the potential threat from near neighbours. They know that Japan, Vietnam and Taiwan stand ready to secure their claim over the disputed islands in the China Seas. India has deployed its substantial navy to block any Chinese moves on the Middle East and their forces on the Himalayan border might try to recover territory lost to China in past conflicts.

North Korea is their only certain ally although we suspect Indonesia may be walking on both sides of the street."

"So, where does that leave us? How safe are we from further attack?"

"We are in a position of military stalemate, Mr President. Our space warfare assets give us nuclear strike supremacy but the degrading of our communications inhibit our capacity to detect their preparations for a first strike launch of their long range missiles. They are aware that this would be suicidal and as long as their leaders remain rational America is safe from attack. In the meanwhile we are working to reactivate our satellite surveillance capability which will take some time."

"Are we then blind to Chinese strategic intentions and how can we get back online again?"

"Not entirely sir. I reported that almost all of our terrestrial communication stations are down but there is one which is still functioning. It relies on older generation technology which has proved to be immune to disruption by cyber-attacks and it is powered by its own nuclear plant. It is enabling us to maintain some contact and communication between our forces in the eastern sphere and a foundation on which we hope to rebuild our global links. The enemy seems unaware of its precise location and it is vital to our security that we keep it operational and free from attack."

"Where is this vital asset?"

"It is located deep underground beneath an ancient mountain

range in a remote and inhospitable place called The Kimberley."

"And where is that?"

"Somewhere in Australia, sir."

2

Somewhere in Australia

Coober Pedy

Australian army engineers had converted a warren of abandoned opal mines, deep under the desert near Coober Pedy, into an undetectable, bomb-proof home for military high command and the war cabinet. Its natural ambient temperature insulated against the fierce daytime summer heat on the surface and the nightly winter frosts. Its approach roads were paved with crushed local rock which left no tell-tale wheel marks and its unobtrusive entrances and exits were indistinguishable from the adits of hundreds of surrounding abandoned and still operational mines.

It was equipped with all the technological wizardry necessary to communicate with and direct land, sea and air forces across Australia's sphere of influence. Inhabitant comforts had not been neglected as evidenced by the depleted glass of ice-cold beer contemplated by Major Glen Jones, with the blissful satisfaction of one long deprived of what he considered to be his birth-right.

"Jeeze, I needed that. It's hot as Hades out there-must be at least fifty degrees in the sun and although we flew most of the way across from Canberra that last bit in the desert cruiser caked my throat with dust."

Captain Frank Bevan, whose tour of duty with Norforce in the Kimberley and his assignment here had acclimatised him to the peculiar demands of life in a desert climate smiled wryly.

"Come off it Glen you always were a whingeing bastard and here you are half way through a life-restoring Cooper's ale. Give a thought to those poor buggers on what they called peacekeeping duties in the Middle East, trying to keep the Sunnis and Shias from each other's throats, sleeping in sand-blasted dongas and subsisting on sweet tea and combat rations. You don't know when you are well off."

"Alright Frank, point taken. Who are those miserable looking bastards in civvies at the far end of the bar?"

"You'll be surprised to know that words are as lethal as bullets coming from our bold political leaders and those lost souls are the remaining remnant of the once almighty Canberra press corps, much depleted and retrenched by the shutdown of TV, radio and their personal blogs. There's a rumour that some former ABC news stars are even trying to launch an old fashioned newspaper."

"Yeah, this communication blackout is having some weird effects. My sister works in the emergency department of a Sydney hospital and she says they are being overwhelmed by teenagers and business types presenting with severe depression at being unable to text, tweet and email. Waste bins are full of discarded mobile phones and for many hysterical young, girls, Facebook is a fading wet dream. Postmen are back on their rounds but letter post is not much help to the many who were never taught to write properly at school."

Before Frank could respond, a Sergeant appeared at their table and announced that the command meeting was about to start and that their presence was required.

In the command centre, the Defence Minister sat with a rank of Generals, Admirals and Air Commodores in an arc facing huge wall-mounted monitors transmitting the full scope of Australia's military deployment, along with occasional coverage of life in the major cities. The centre drew its power from a dedicated nuclear reactor. Although the financially crippling and technologically superseded communication system known as the National

Broadband Network or NBN had long been abandoned in favour of wireless and satellite links, major government and strategic military sites were still connected by it. They enjoyed email, video and voice over internet services that could only be interrupted by physical attacks which, so far, had not happened

"Ladies and Gentlemen the Prime Minister has spoken with the President of the United States and has asked me to bring you up to speed on developments in the warfare that has broken out in North Asia and Russia's Far East. Major Jones is a senior analyst from Military Intelligence whose responsibilities cover that region and he will update you on the current state of hostilities."

"Thank you Minister. Ladies and gentlemen you are familiar with most of what has happened as a result of China's cyber-attacks and military incursion into Russia. So I will confine my comments to our immediate situation, but please ask any questions you might have at any time.

"In a nutshell, China has achieved its main strategic aim of securing Russia's Eastern Siberian energy resources for its own use, replacing those it has lost as a result of the Middle East war. By employing first strike cyber-attacks they have rendered Russia powerless to defend itself but, due to the superiority of American cyber defences and their revelation of hitherto secret space-based nuclear missile capabilities, an armed stalemate exists between China the U.S. and its allies, including ourselves. American naval forces have incurred minor damage. The European Republic is in total disarray due to disruption of its unprotected computer-dependent systems. Japan and South Korea which are under the American shield, have achieved a position of armed neutrality towards Chinese ships and aircraft passing through their sea lanes and air corridors, on their way to annex Russian Oil and Gas.

That brings me to our situation. As you know our major cities are running on severely reduced power and are without telecommunications. We are working to restore these as soon as possible and in the interim, martial law has been declared throughout Australia. Our decision to lease long-range nuclear-powered submarines from the Americans and arm them with nuclear tipped missiles has dissuaded the Chinese from encroaching on our northern energy resources and as we are also part of the U.S. alliance, we have ceased all shipments of coal, gas, uranium and food to China."

"That is a helpful summary of where we are at Major, but where do we go from here?"

"Admiral, the key to restoring total military deterrence is to get the chain of global defence communication satellites and ground relay stations back on the air. In this respect we have a critical role to play as the only currently functioning relay station is one of ours, up in the Kimberley. This is enabling some coordination and communication of our and our allies' forces and so far, the Chinese have been unable to silence it and may not have even detected it yet. That is the limit of my remit and so I will hand you back to the Defence Minister."

"Thank you Major and now I fear that I shall have to close this meeting as further deliberation into our next steps, particularly the defence of the Kimberley Station, must be discussed and approved by the war cabinet. Until then all reference to this facility and its role must be deemed top secret."

Back in the bar Frank congratulated Glen on his presentation.

"Well done, Glen. You certainly gave them something to think about and I guess the Kimberley is going to get more attention than it did when the prospectors and greenies fought over it back in 013. Now you must really have a dry throat and as it's my shout what's your pleasure?"

Melbourne

Shattered window glass from the burnt-out skeletons of looted shops carpeted the streets. Litter and uncollected mounds of rotting garbage blocked city pavements and subsided into the streets. Lifeless trams, electric cars and trucks stood abandoned in the middle of roadways and at intersections, where their power supply had run out. There was no sign of human life because of the nightly curfew but dogs were beginning to hunt in packs. Darkness and unearthly silence shrouded the city. Melbourne seemed barely alive.

Wincing every time his bicycle's wheels crunched on shards of glass and praying that he would not suffer a puncture, Ibrahim rode steadily towards the sanctuary of a blacked-out mosque. He was responding to an important summons but although a devout Muslim, he was not answering a call to prayer.

Ibrahim had lived in Melbourne for many years, since arriving as a young student on an Australian Government sponsored scholarship to study engineering at Monash University. He had prospered and so enjoyed the lifestyle and career opportunities that he had taken out citizenship and joined the Federal Public Service. His good looks, laid-back manner and excellent English made it easy for him to make friends and his diligence and skills earned the respect of his work mates. His superiors recognised his professional capability and with the increasing necessity of trading and negotiating with Australia's northern neighbour, his fluency in English and Bahasa Indonesia was especially valued and had boosted his steady promotion to his present senior position, in an area responsible for international telecommunications regulations.

Despite living in Australia for most of his adult life he had spent his formative years in Indonesia, where his extended family still lived and his divided loyalties tilted more readily towards his Asian homeland. This had never been a problem for him until war had broken out in the region and he had received an invitation from the Indonesian Embassy to attend a meeting at a Melbourne mosque.

The dimly lit room to which the caretaker escorted him had all the trappings of a gentleman's study and he assumed it served as the Imam's office. A tall elegantly-suited man rose from his seat behind a beautiful rosewood desk and initiated the traditional greetings.

"Assalamu aleikum!"

"Wa aleikum assalam!"

With this formality out of the way the stranger invited Ibrahim to seat himself in a well-worn leather arm chair and to listen to what his host had to say.

"Thank you for coming at such short notice and despite the inconvenient curfew restrictions. I will dispense with formalities. All you need to know at this time is that I am a senior member of the Indonesian Diplomatic Service, based in Canberra, and you have my assurance that what I have to say is endorsed by the highest levels of my government in Djakarta.

Whilst Indonesia's public response to the conflicts in the region to our north is one of neutrality, you will know that our security and continuing economic growth are closely linked with the fortunes of China. Ethnic and expatriate Chinese occupy very influential positions in the highest levels of our society and without their know-how and capital investment we would not have grown as fast as we have. For these reasons and because we need to restore a reliable source of energy supply after the disruptions in the Middle East, we are under great pressure to cooperate with the Chinese and to assist them in any way we can, despite our not declaring a preference for either of the opposing alliances."

Ibrahim listened intently, even though what was being said was no surprise and was in tune with both his own appreciation of his country's predicament and his personal sympathies. He doubted the man's identification as a diplomatic officer. He certainly dressed the part and spoke with appropriately silky eloquence. But his direct manner and penetrating gaze suggested a more sinister and ruthless occupation. He suspected that this anonymous government servant was really an officer with the BIN or Badan Intelijen Negara, the much feared Indonesian Intelligence service. He dreaded what might have brought him to their attention and resolved it was time to find out why they had summoned him.

"I appreciate your frank account of our country's position.

It is no great surprise to me and under the current circumstances I am sympathetic with our government's strategic leaning. But as I have been so long absent from Indonesia I fail to see what this has to do with me."

"In fact, a great deal Ibrahim, as I shall explain to you. You will be aware that hostilities have occurred, mainly between Chinese and Russian forces and to a lesser extent involving the United States. Overwhelming Chinese force and America's technological edge are all but cancelling each other out, giving neither a winning advantage at this stage. The disruption of communications between U.S. global satellite links and ground relay stations is critical to China's defences but it appears that the Americans still have a small but vital capability to coordinate its force projection, as evidenced by their successful missile attack on a Chinese fleet, even after they had lost their main communication and guidance systems.

The Chinese do not know precisely where this remaining operational facility is located but they do know that it is somewhere in Australia and they have called on us to help them find and destroy it. That Ibrahim is where you come in and why your government needs your help."

Ibrahim cycled away from the mosque trusting to the darkness and his keeping to suburban streets and back lanes to avoid running into curfew roadblocks. He had agreed to use his position to try to identify the precise location of the operational relay station, mostly on account of his sympathy for Indonesia's cause but also because the agent's detailed knowledge about his family back home threatened bad consequences for them if he had not assented.

3

Somewhere in the Kimberley

Bungle Bungle base

It seemed somewhat bizarre to all who served there that Australia's most technically advanced and futuristic defence communications base should have been sited deep underground in the Kimberley wilderness, concealed beneath the protective strata of some of the oldest rock formations on earth. Although situated in a remote corner of the popular Purnalulu National Park, signs on its perimeter fence warned of dangers and severe consequences that would befall trespassers on a well-known international minerals company's diamond mine site. It was a self-contained facility, even boasting its own runway, so that all necessary supplies and personnel flew in and out, presumably from Darwin or even Perth. There was no contact with surrounding cattle stations and nobody, including the few remaining Aboriginal people who hunted and went walk-about outside its perimeter, either knew or cared what was going on inside the fenced-off zone. Grey nomad trailer-home travellers from the southern cities showed occasional curiosity but park rangers claimed ignorance and did nothing to encourage their enquiries. In the wet season it was free of such prying eyes and now that wartime restrictions on travel to and across the north were in force, unauthorised ground traffic was denied access.

Under cover of darkness the high-speed helo-jet swooped in and descended silently onto the base's landing pad. The passengers, consisting of a small party of military chiefs and senior bureaucrats with the highest security clearance, were met by the base's visitor vetting team and ushered out of the chill outback night air and into a high-speed elevator that would plunge them on a stomach-churning journey down into the depths far beneath the mountain. The delegation had been tasked to ensure the base remained undetected by the enemy and defensible against all possible attacks.

The base commander greeted them in his uniform of pristine white shorts and shirt whose insignia and display of medal ribbons testified to his elevated rank, long service and bravery in former wars. He made no apology for the immediate start of their familiarisation program, despite the late hour and their long journey.

"Good evening. I hope you have at least managed to enjoy a refreshing shower and change. I appreciate that you will be tired and perhaps hungry after your long flight but in this emergency situation I am under strict orders to allow nothing to delay your mission. Your overview of the base's purpose and capability will commence immediately and whilst I can do nothing to alleviate your fatigue, an endless supply of good strong coffee will be at hand and our canteen has prepared a sustaining if somewhat fattening range of finger-food, much favoured by our service men and women, including pies, sausage rolls, burgers, chicken drumsticks and kebabs, complete with all sauces from peanut to tomato."

Growls of satisfaction greeted this welcome offering and as soon as their cups were filled and plates loaded, the hungry, weary, but alert audience prepared for their first briefing.

To their surprise and heightened interest their presenter was not the expected , male, military officer but a tall and willowy brown-skinned woman with dark piercing eyes and shoulder length hair that spilled over the collar of her white, starched lab coat. Kate Carew was a scientist, not a soldier. She knew her stuff and was not afraid to use the beauty born of her indigenous heritage to grab their attention and get her message across.

"Welcome to Bungle Bungle Base. I will not be going into the advanced technical aspects of the technologies employed here but I am happy to answer any of your questions about this at the end of the presentation. This base is the last remaining operational link in a global chain of communication satellites and ground-based relay stations, designed to provide detection and early warning of potential enemy aggression. It is designed to coordinate and direct counter strikes by land, sea and air forces and from inner space stations. My focus will be on what we can and cannot do.

You are aware that Chinese attacks have severely degraded the performance of the total U.S. system but most importantly this Australian owned and operated base is still fully operational. We cannot provide the global reach of the undamaged system but we can monitor military movements in North Asia, detect impending attacks from that region, provide targeting information for American space-launched missiles and command and control of our own military forces. Initial Chinese cyber-attacks did not shut us down and it seems that whilst they are aware of us they do not have our precise location."

"Why aren't they able to locate and disable the base?"

"For a combination of reasons General. We employ older technology than the Americans and it seemed to be impervious to the attacks which silenced their facilities and disabled our cities. They could only put us out of action with a direct physical attack but we are far away, deep under a protective mountain range and they don't know where we are. As to why they have not detected our precise location, it could be something to do with the shielding effect of the rock strata above. These are amongst the oldest geological formations in the world and they are rich in a diverse range of minerals and energy sources, such as diamonds, gold and uranium. Not to mention the protective power of the dreamtime spirits."

This last remark was said with a fleeting smile and her audience were left wondering how seriously it was meant to be taken.

"There is one more thing I want to share with you gentlemen which will be very useful to you in coming days and which must be kept totally secret. It is an Australian development which has not yet been shared with our allies. We have developed a psycho-electronic form of communication which we call Thought-Mail orT-M for short. It operates person to person in the same way that SMS and e-mail do with the difference that it transmits voice messages which arrive as thoughts in the mind of the recipient."

"My God, Kate this sounds to me like pure science fiction. How does it work?"

"I was equally sceptical, Admiral, when I first heared about it but I have used it and it works. I am afraid that I am not allowed to tell you how it works but, it requires the insertion of a tiny transmitter-receiver node into the head of users. This is done surgically under local anaesthetic and appears to have no detrimental effect on those who have used it. The system cannot be hacked into and is immune to any known method of interference but its operational range is limited. We believe it could be most effective in maintaining communication between commanders and field patrols, where very short and precise messages are involved.

So, it is vital that we remain operational and retain our anonymity. The commander will deal with the military aspects of this."

"Thank you Kate. In case you thought she was kidding about protective spirits, her father is the most senior elder of the local Aboriginal tribe, with responsibility for guarding and maintaining the painted rock-art image of the Wandjina, whose powers protect this land. We have sought to deceive the enemy about the source of our signals by relaying them via reconnaissance drones and nuclear submarines, which are constantly changing positions. We are able to intercept any possible aerial attack and all but a nuclear payload would be unable to penetrate our mountain ceiling. A major ground assault would be detected long before a landing could be made in Australia and it would be a sitting duck in the open terrain that surrounds the Bungle Bungle ranges."

"But Commander, as the Chinese have demonstrated their ability to disable or at least disrupt our communications, what if their ground forces were able to evade electronic detection?"

"Good question sir. In that event we would fall back on the traditional trip-wire warning that worked so well in the war against Imperial Japan. We have maintained the Norforce regiments and as I speak they are mounting on-going reconnaissance patrols across the north. Although the majority of our regular troops are deployed to maintain order during the current crises in our cities, a ready reaction force is available from Darwin on twenty-four hour standby. We have arranged for you to meet the local Norforce units and to observe their training and operations.Captain Frank Bevan, who is attached to your party, has served with Norforce and he is here to assist you in liaising with its units and assessing their capabilities and readiness."

Wandjina dreamtime

Kate Carew enjoyed her position as chief scientific officer at the Defence Satellite Communications base deep in the Kimberley wilderness. She was proud of what she had achieved since leaving school in Perth and of her aboriginal heritage. Without the support of her family and community, which sacrificed funds from their mining royalties to finance her educational journey via Perth to her graduation in cyber-maths at the Australian National University she could not have succeeded. She had been happy in her early career roles with the Commonwealth Scientific and Industrial Research Organisation but the time spent at Massachusetts Institute of Technology on a NASA scholarship had broadened her skills and career horizons and this had not escaped the notice of the Australian Government.

She had jumped at the offer of a posting with Defence Science and the heaven-sent opportunity to continue her cutting-edge work in satellite cryptography, whilst living in her people's ancestral home land. It had gone a long way to healing the rift that had opened up between these conflicting choices and which had been torn further apart by her experience of a full-on life in America and the painful end of a short and torrid love affair. It was a continuing joy and wonder to be able to balance and combine the futuristic work of satellite encryption with her leisure-time indulgence in the arcane lore of outback hunting; surviving on bush tucker and visiting the sacred rock art sites created by her distant forebears that few women were allowed to see.

She had not been joking when she referred to guardian spirits protecting the land on which the base stood. Her father, as senior elder and leader of her tribe, was charged with the responsibility of maintaining ancient symbolic paintings of the Wandjina cloud and rain spirits on rock walls, where it was believed they had died and entered a nearby water hole. They were reputed to have the power to bring the life-preserving monsoon rains and to punish those who broke the law by bringing floods, lightening and cyclones. Had she not seen the terror that could be invoked in the minds of Aboriginal tribal law breakers by projecting the punitive powers of the Wandjinas onto them, often leading to their death, she would not have given any credence to these claims and dismissed them as pure mythology.

4

The Enemy Within

Melbourne

Ibrahim knew that the secret communications station would be tightly guarded and under military control. But because of the technology it would need to use he figured that there would have to be a link with civilian telecommunication authorities and it would need access to high level scientists and technicians. Whilst comforted by this reasoning his initial research had drawn a blank. All he could ascertain from his staff and professional contacts was that upon outbreak of hostilities, large numbers of specialists had been drafted into the defence forces and whilst most were engaged in trying to resist and recover from cyber-attacks, some had gone out of circulation, presumably to join units engaged in top secret work in unknown locations.

Discreet enquiries had failed to reveal any of these destinations. Their friends and families were unaware of their location and the most senior managers in his department did not know or would not tell where their brightest and best had disappeared to. Legitimate lines of enquiry at departmental meetings got him nowhere. Technical equipment procurement and supply records did not tell the full story. Records of outgoing quantities and inventories held in store did not tally with the considerably greater orders fulfilled by manufacturers and locations to which the gear had been despatched. Details of the recipients were not recorded.

He was under growing pressure from his controller in Canberra to come up with the required information and he was becoming desperately afraid for both his own safety and that of his family if he were to fail. It was clear that lines of conventional enquiry would not work, especially as the people in the know were subject to the severe penalties of the wartime Official Secrets Act and ASIO officers, both in the open and under cover, maintained a tight watch on where they went and who they met with. He was untrained and unaided in this work. In moments of desperation, verging on panic, he wondered whether he would ever succeed. In a calmer state of mind he knew there must be informal ways of breaching the security cordon but what they were and how to access them, he did not know.

It was as a result of a chance conversation with a Muslim friend after prayers at the mosque, that his eyes were opened to new lines of enquiry. The man was a relative newcomer to Australia and had sought Ibrahim's advice on settling in.

"Ibrahim, how can an outsider like me get to know Australians better and become more accepted into non-Muslim social circles?"

"Your question, my friend, contains the key to how you can fit in better. It is natural for you as a newcomer to attach yourself to people who think like you but if you are to be more readily accepted by the wider Australian community you must be prepared to go where they congregate and try as much as possible to do what they do. For instance, to get to know the men, you need to show some interest in their favourite sports which might involve going to football matches, adopting a team to support or trying to play golf. They meet and celebrate in pubs and bars and even though they drink alcohol they will respect and accept your decision to stick to soft drink, as long as you give them good reason, drink with them and pay your round. Also it is easier to make women friends here. The men will introduce you and it is acceptable to meet them at dance clubs without chaperones."

Ibrahim accepted his friend's thanks and thought no more of

this exchange until he lay in bed mulling over the day's events and what little progress he had made when suddenly, he realised that an obvious answer to his dilemma was to follow his own advice. He had to mix with and befriend those people most likely to know something that would lead him to identify the location of the secret base.

This did not require a radical change of behaviour. Ibrahim had chosen to cheer for the Collingwood "Magpies" Australian Rules Football team and he had learned enough of the game's rules and backgrounds of the star players to hold his own in lunchtime and barroom debates and arguments. He was a more than competent squash player and his dark, handsome looks, lithe physique and quiet attentive manner had more than charmed a number of ladies to open their arms and legs to him and enticed them into his bed. His anxiety gave way to enthusiastic contemplation of strategies that would be both enjoyable to implement and likely to get the result he so desperately needed.

The Watchers

Jane Smith had been given less than eight hours' notice to catch the first available flight from Melbourne to Canberra and present herself at the offices of the Defence Intelligence Organisation. She had been kept waiting for over an hour in a dingy reception area in their headquarters and her patience was running out when she received the summons to a top-floor office. Judging by the higher standard of décor at this elevation she rightly concluded that this was where the upper échelons dwelled. This assumption was confirmed by the seniority of the uniformed officer who faced her across his huge mahogany desk. Her immediate instinct was to come to attention and deliver a smart salute but, as she was no longer a serving soldier, she was saved from the embarrassment of her indecisive stance by his leaning forward, offering her a very firm handshake and welcoming her to his office in a voice remarkable for its deep, dark, velvet tones.

"G'day, Miss Smith. Please take a seat. Thank you for coming at such short notice. It was necessary because of the serious and urgent nature of what I have to tell you." As she sat, the door to an adjoining office opened and a steward appeared bearing a silver-service tray containing a large coffee pot, two cups and a selection of delicate triangular sandwiches. "This will take a while and I thought you might appreciate some sustenance after the junk, masquerading as food, the airlines serve." She was indeed peckish and the coffee smelled divine. It was the real thing.

"Thank you sir, I am ready for some refreshment and although I am curious as to why I have been called to come here in such a hurry I expect it will be best if I let you start and save my questions for later."

He assured her that this was his preference and launched into his explanation.

"Before I start, whilst you are no longer subject to military discipline I understand that you are governed by the Official Secrets Act in your current position and I must stress that what I am about to say must be kept absolutely secret and only to be discussed between you and me."

Jane fully understood the restriction placed on her. After a five year stint in the Australian Army, most of which involved postings in South-East Asia where her degree in Asian studies and command of Bahasa Indonesia had been fully utilised, she had been seconded to The Australian Secret Intelligence Service. She had successfully completed assignments which required her to work under cover and which exposed her to considerable danger. Her training had been thorough and her skills included the ability to defend herself by using unconventional methods that could be fatal for any adversary. Also, she was a crack shot with hand guns, could handle a machine pistol as well as any special forces, soldier and knew much more uses for knives than her surgeon father had ever dreamed of.

"We have picked up intelligence that members of the supposedly neutral Indonesian Embassy staff have been snooping around more than usually in places where they might learn about our defence communications capabilities and dispositions. We do not know yet why they are doing this, or what they are trying to find out. At official diplomatic level their declared neutrality has been accepted by our government. But there are suspicions that their dependence on the influential Chinese diaspora living in Indonesia and their fear of being cut off from secure Middle Eastern energy supplies, is causing them to maintain good relations with China and we know of regular clandestine meetings between their military and intelligence leaderships.

We suspect that officers of Badan Intelijen Negara are posing as embassy officials and one in particular has been spotted making periodic visits to a Melbourne mosque outside the normal hours of worship. So far so good, but this is where everything you hear becomes classified. There is a secret the Chinese would dearly like to know and it is the location of our only operational Defence Communications base. They must be prevented from acquiring this information at all costs and you have been seconded to this department to help us frustrate their spies."

"I am flattered to be considered for such a critical assignment, but why me?"

"You have relevant training, the required linguistic skills and you have operated in Indonesia. You are a Melburnian and that is where Indonesian agents are fishing for information. Finally, you are known to be a member of the Telecommunications Department organisation and a woman, which makes you more likely to be underestimated and overlooked by Islamic men."

"Well I guess some of that is a testament to my capabilities. So when do you want me to start and what do you want me to do?"

"We want you to start immediately by returning to Melbourne and after a briefing from my officers there, you should start moving in the same circles where foreign agents are trawling for information."

5

Standing By

Somewhere in China

The camel train swung along a little used desert track which had once formed part of an ancient spice route. But trade was not their purpose and this mode of transport had long been made redundant by the construction of a sealed highway across this part of the Taklamakan Desert in North Western China. The beasts were heavily laden with panniers full of small arms, ammunition and explosives and were bound for a secret military training base in a remote corner of this harsh and arid terrain.

They had been going all day and both animals and cameleers were weary and welcomed the cooling effect of the incoming desert night. As they descended through a narrow defile, just three miles from their destination, the men's thoughts were on the prospect of a splash in cool water, hot food and refreshing tea to wash away the dust lining their parched throats.

Without warning the sand beside the trail erupted as though ripped apart by silent explosives and six heavily-armed men, with camouflaged faces and desert-toned combat suits burst out, overpowered the camel drivers and trussed them up with thin nylon ropes. Although the captives were local Uyghurs familiar with the desert and also as well trained Chinese army commandos, they had failed to anticipate the ambush and the attackers had achieved total surprise.

Later that evening in the officers' mess, back at the base, the Chinese Army Commandant raised his glass of rice wine and led a toast to the Indonesian Kopassus special-forces unit, in recognition of their skill in carrying out a perfect ambush in such unfamiliar terrain. He was especially impressed with the length of time they had endured waiting under the hot sand with only reed straws to breathe through. Captain Abdul Supomo stood, raising his glass of green tea in response and accepted the compliment with quiet modesty.

Indonesia's Kopassus special-forces units trained to carry out operations similar to those undertaken by British and Australian SAS and were expected to be able to operate efficiently in all manner of climates and terrains. But, even if Indonesia was to become involved in China's war with Russia, Abdul wondered why he and his men had been assigned to exercise in the dry conditions of a desert whose name meant 'the point of no return', when the war in the north was being fought in Siberia's icy wastes.

He was a dedicated soldier, proud of achieving a leadership role in such a legendary force and committed totally to the service of the modern Republic of Indonesia. He understood that the great strides his country had achieved in reducing the formerly endemic poverty owed much to the technical and financial contribution of its Chinese citizens and their motherland. The past alliance with the Americans and their Asian allies had also been good in that it had facilitated the growth of trade with western countries and offered technical education to a rapidly growing younger generation of Indonesians. Now the Americans relied on their own energy sources and their diplomatic neglect had failed to prevent the Middle East war cutting off oil and gas supplies which stifled the economic growth of emerging Asian powers. He could see why his government was hedging its bets by declaring neutrality whilst maintaining secret negotiations with the Chinese government. It was vital that Indonesia was on the winning side after the war.

But he had been raised a muslim and having to side with the

heathen Chinese caused him a great degree of anguish and doubt. He had taken the problem to his Imam and the advice he received had largely eased this disquiet.

"In a perfect world my son you would be right to refuse to associate with the godless Chinese but the alternative of hanging on to the coat-tails of the Christian Americans is only marginally better because of our exclusive belief in and loyalty to Allah. Whatever the outcome of this war, we must not end up on the losing side as this would pose a great danger to the continuing survival of Islam. It is for this reason alone, that our religious leaders have given their blessing to our President's double game and I am happy to condone your commitment to this duty, despite our personal misgivings."

Djakarta

"Foreign Minister, has there been any progress in discovering the exact location of the Australian communications base?"

"Not exactly sir. Our intelligence agents are seeking to penetrate the code of secrecy imposed on Australians involved in high level telecommunications and we have been successful in recruiting an Indonesian born engineer who holds a very senior executive position in the Australian Public Service department responsible for this industry."

"I am sure you appreciate the urgency with which the Chinese await our success. What are your plans for acting on this information as soon as we obtain it?"

"Indeed Mr President, our military planners have advised that even if we locate the base in Australia we could not launch a successful aerial attack and so the only way to put it out of action requires a ground assault. This could only be done by a small clandestine force that could get to the base undetected or at least not until they had completed the sabotage."

"You are proposing a suicide mission by our special forces?"

"I am afraid that is likely to be the outcome of even a successful incursion. In anticipation of this we have assumed that the station is located far from urban areas and most likely in some remote part of what Australians call their 'outback'. With this in mind, we have sent a top Kopassus unit to train in a Chinese desert area which will give them experience of operating in conditions of fierce daytime heat, freezing nights and where water is extremely hard to locate. It is under the command of our most decorated special-forces officer and the reports I am receiving suggest that their performance has certainly impressed and reassured the Chinese that the team can cope with the worst they would experience in the Australian wilderness areas."

"That is good news. Keep me informed of progress and let me know when our agents have found where the base is."

6

Spy Hunt

Marvellous Melbourne

Her cocktail was complex and cold but the jazz was primitive and very hot. Jane made a visual sweep of the crowded club whilst seeming to be focused only on sampling her drink. She loved Melbourne, which like a late opening flower had continued to blossom into the most liveable of cities, whilst Sydney withered and had fallen further behind. The second catastrophic global banking crisis, sparked by the collapse of the Euro, had destroyed the finance industry on which it depended and emptied the casinos leaving it no more than a latter day harbour-side theme park, just a city attached to a bay. Here in Richmond, she lived and played and so did the bright young things from the telecommunications industry amongst whom, the secret information sought by the enemy could be found.

Jane Smith was reared and educated in Melbourne and she felt so lucky to be able to return to pursue her career in such a vibrant and cosmopolitan city. Her surgeon father had insisted on her getting the best of educational opportunities and he was pleased to finance her time at Methodist Ladies College where she had excelled both academically and in sport. He and her mother had hoped she might follow in his footsteps and tread a medical path but Jane was too addicted to action to spend hours in consulting rooms or sterile operating theatres. Her thirst for adventure and travel took her to Asia, where she completed her university education and, to her parents' horror, joined the Army.

She did not take readily to its insistence on dutiful obedience and the rigid routines. But she learned so many valuable skills, especially how to hold her own in a man's world, defend herself against greater physical strength and in extremity, how to kill. Her progression into the officer ranks had been rapid but when her individuality and larrikin behaviour seemed to be stalling further promotion, intelligence agencies came knocking at her door. They swept her off into a completely different world where initiative and individual achievement were the keys to success. Assignments had been both top secret and very dangerous. She had worked under cover and some of the things she had done and the perils she had survived still gave her nightmares.

A tangled mass of dancers surged to and fro across the club's dance floor. There was a fairly equal distribution of men and women whose mixed national and racial origins befitted a migration melting pot. It was not easy to single out possible Indonesian agents and she knew that Caucasians might have been recruited to the Indon-Chinese cause. But she knew which of the dancers were privy to information about the Kimberley base and she concentrated on their partners and especially those who were paying them close attention.

One in particular stood out, a tall, good-looking guy, who seemed to know all the right dance moves and the smiles on his partners' faces, when he swept them into his embrace, suggested this was not his only charm. Jane decided he might be worth getting to know.

7

Deadly Force

Making its mark

After the briefing about the base, Frank escorted the visitors to a training area not far from the park's boundary where Norforce officers and men were being put through their paces. The formation was tasked with surveillance and reconnaissance duties across the north and north-west of Australia and had grown out of the fledgling North Australia Observation Unit, nicknamed the Nackaroos or Curtin's Cowboys, which had been scrambled together in 1942 in response to the threat of Japanese invasion.

A high proportion of its recruits were local Aboriginals and in addition to their natural ability to navigate and subsist in the harsh Kimberley climate and terrain, their training with the closely allied SAS had equipped them with the same fighting capabilities as that elite outfit. Frank had told the visiting group about the history and operational prowess of the regiment before inviting them to accompany him and a few Norforce officers for a walk onto their training area.

"Gentlemen, it is hard to gain a real appreciation of what these soldiers can do without going out with them on an extended patrol and so what you will see today will be a small demonstration of their capability."

For the next two hours the Norforce men put on an impressive display of stalking, individual and collective firepower, canyon wall scaling and improvised crossing of a monsoon-swollen river, using their packs as floats. As the party walked back along the rocky bed of a dry boulder-strewn creek, which was devoid of covering by scrub, grass and trees. A General voiced his concern about their ability to take an enemy by surprise in such open country.

"That was impressive Bevan, they can certainly spot and track an enemy patrol but how can they mount a surprise attack when there is no natural cover from which to mount an ambush?"

"Glad you mentioned that General," Frank replied drawing a whistle from his pocket and blowing three sharp blasts.

Explosions and a pall of smoke disoriented and engulfed the party which was enveloped by a large net, cast down on them by a hovering mortar drone. Confused but unharmed the captives were amazed to see the very rocks of the creek bed rise up and assume the form of cunningly camouflaged soldiers who were armed to the teeth and glared at them ferociously. Spared the indignity of being trussed like chickens and forced to lie face down on the rock, the stunned visitors were released from the net and escorted with the greatest concern for their welfare and profuse apologies for the liberty the commandos had taken with them to make their point. Recovery of their hearing and decorum was greatly speeded by the serving of copious drafts of champagne and artfully flavoured, barbecued seafood and meats, courtesy of the regimental caterers in an air-conditioned marquee. After a while the highest ranking visitor rose to speak and propose a toast

"I must say Bevan that was the most disconcerting and damned effective military demonstration I have ever attended and if I might misquote the Duke of Wellington – as they so easily deceived and frightened old campaigners like us, by God they will certainly terrify the enemy. Gentlemen charge your glasses, be upstanding and drink a toast to Norforce in whose hands we can confidently place responsibility for protecting our base from attack."

As the last of the guests weaved their merry way back to their transport, the General in charge of Norforce operations across the whole of northern Australia, drew Frank aside and asked,

"Captain Bevan, I have a great interest in our military history. Please tell me am I wrong or is it a remarkable coincidence that a descendant of the celebrated Dan Bevan, who performed so heroically with Norforce during the Japanese war, should be here today when we face a similar risk of invasion?"

"No sir, you are not mistaken. He is an ancestor of mine and I was raised on stories of his bravery and ability to fight and survive in the harshest and most dangerous Kimberley country. He is revered in the family and is buried with his equally heroic wife, Liza Bevan, not far from here on our family's cattle station."

"Thank you Bevan for confirming that. I am sure you will not be called on to confront the dreadful hardships and dangers he overcame with such courage and disregard for his own survival."

"No sir, as they say back in Coober Pedy where I am based, one is more likely to be wounded by a paper cut there than by a bullet or bayonet."

"Thanks for your help in impressing the brass and good luck!"

8
Loose Lips

To lure a tiger

Jane reported back to her controller what she had learned at the jazz club. The women who had been approached by possible foreign agents could recall no untoward questioning by their partners and whilst the man called Ibrahim had not mentioned communications facilities, he had danced with all of the most informed women and had interrogated them intensely about where they worked and what they did.

"Jane, it's time to stake-out the goat to tempt the tiger."

"Yes, I thought it might come to that. Well, if I am to be the bait I expect there to be plenty of your big-game hunters standing by ready to rescue me if the tiger is peckish."

"Don't worry. We have you under close surveillance at all times and I understand that you are no slouch when it comes to defending yourself."

"True. But one always has to prepare for the unexpected and I would feel better with some of your heavy mob riding shotgun."

"Go for it. We've got your back."

Over the next few days false information about Jane's role in the organisation was leaked onto the grapevine including vague hints that she was working on something top secret involving communications technology. A search of Ibrahim's background threw up no incriminating evidence but the details of his interests and hobbies proved very useful. In addition to the leaking of information to attract him, if he were a spy, Jane began to leave her own trail of lures to draw him to her.

She visited the Melbourne mosque with which the Indonesian intelligence officer had been associated and made enquiries about how one converted to Islam and came away with a pile of literature and a copy of the Koran. She too was a keen squash player and having joined the same club at which Ibrahim played she arranged to showcase her style and skills at times when he was up in the viewing gallery.

His reaction was swift. He contrived to meet her, seemingly by chance, in the department canteen. After he had asked about her work and met a veil of consistent evasion his enquiries switched to other topics unrelated to telecommunications.

"I saw you at the squash club the other day and it looks as though you have played quite a bit."

"Yes. I took it up at school and represented my university for a while. But now I am too busy with my work to train seriously and so I only play socially."

"We should play a game some time. Perhaps one evening this week and the winner can pay for dinner?"

"That would be nice," Jane said, giving Ibrahim an encouraging smile. "I am free on Tuesday. Perhaps you will book a court?"

"You can count on it. See you at six o'clock and bring your best game."

"Be sure I will and I look forward to dining sumptuously at your expense."

Closing in

They met at the Department's courts which were lit by power from an assured government source of supply. The squash match was hard fought and Ibrahim's arrogant assumption that he would soon prevail was dashed by Jane's speed after the ball and the power and pin-point accuracy of her shots just above the tin. He was soon lathered in sweat and a small crowd had gathered to watch as word got round that a woman was giving him a run for his money. It took all of his skill and guile to remain in contention and just when it seemed he would lose Jane took her foot off the gas, muffed a few critical shots and feigning exhaustion, conceded the match.

Ibrahim was exhilarated by the contest and not a little triumphant at having prevailed over this smart and athletic woman. He felt so good that despite his winning he insisted that dinner would be on him.

He had chosen to take her to Melbourne's best Indonesian restaurant, which somehow, despite supply rationing, still managed to serve more than passable food. The candle-lit alcove he had booked was ideal for his seductive intentions. Jane played along allowing him to take masterful charge of ordering the food and selecting a complementary non-alcoholic wine, which didn't taste at all bad.

As they ate and talked the focus of his conversation became more and more personal and increasingly intimate. He felt sure that she knew where the base was and that he was going to enjoy seducing the information out of her. Jane was equally pleased with the way the conversation was going and as in the squash match she carefully concealed her best shots and only unleashed her most cunning and un-returnable lob when the waiter came to take their order for desserts.

Before he could consult the menu and suggest what they might have next, Jane stunned and delighted him by ordering his favourite sweet in perfect Bahasa Indonesia. For a brief moment he was lost for words and then thanked her in his native tongue for ordering a dish which his mother used to make for him as a special treat.

"How wonderful. You speak the language so fluently and with a Javanese accent. How did this come about?"

"I have always been fascinated with all things Asian and I won a Colombo-style scholarship to study in Indonesia and the course included Bahasa Indonesia."

Ibrahim was elated and stepped up his schmoozing technique. His honeyed words flowed more sweetly from his lips when spoken in his own language and finally, when she agreed to accompany him back to his place to hear some Gamelan music, he knew he was on a winner. Correspondingly, despite her seemingly compliant and simpering surrender, Kate knew that the Tiger had taken the bait.

His style was smooth and well-practiced. A one-handed unsnapping of her bra strap, a Houdini-like shedding of all his clothes, a slow, oh so smooth, unpeeling of her remaining garments and he took her into his bed. He was in good shape and his body was both firmly muscled and so silky to her touch. For a moment she responded eagerly to his foreplay, stroking his ever so rampant cock and gently cupping his inflated balls. He reached down and with delicate caresses teased and probed the wet lips of her opening flower. As she parted her legs to receive him, he grasped them, locking them around his waist and arched his back to add power to his thrust. But before he could enter her, he felt a sharp, excruciating pain in his arse and a trickle of blood flowed down his leg as Jane pricked him several times with her razor-sharp stiletto.

He couldn't grasp what was happening and when she flipped him onto his back and nicked his throat with her knife he called out to his God and feared his life was over. But Jane's knife probes were not intended to kill him but rather to encourage him to talk. It was soon apparent that he was an unwilling and not particularly brave spy and when she had forced him to lie spread-eagled on the bed and tied his arms and legs to the bedposts, she only had to shave the finest sliver of flesh from his foreskin to make him howl for mercy and eagerly confess all that he knew.

She listened intently to his tale of recruitment, coercion and blackmail by Indonesian Intelligence and she was beginning to feel sorry for him when he told her,

"I am glad that you have unmasked me and relieved me of my burden of deceit and dishonour, but I'm afraid you may be too late to protect your secret."

''What do you mean by too late?" Jane hissed.

"There is another woman from the department who I was convinced had the information we needed and I passed her name on to my controller at the embassy and he told me not to bother any more about her as they would take care of her."

''When was this and why then were you pursuing me?"

"I thought you would be able to confirm my assumptions about her and I must confess that I am more than a little attracted to you. I gave them her name and address before I came to meet you for dinner this evening and I expect they will have picked her up by now and have started to question her."

"Oh my God", Jane yelled, "What have you done?" and cutting his bonds, she flung his clothes at him, ordering him to dress and directed him to take her to where she lives."

The word is out

There was no answer to Jane's persistent ringing of the flat's bell. She was either not there or they were working on her in the blacked-out apartment. She had called for back-up and as promised an armed response team was on its way. They had stepped back from the entrance to the apartment block and Jane was desperately considering what to do next when a voice from the intercom abused them for coming again to pester Alice when she had already told them that she had gone to the jazz club, earlier that evening. A quick exchange of short questions and equally terse answers ascertained that this was a neighbour who had told some earlier callers where they might find Alice. She couldn't see them but they were male and sounded rather like Chinese.

The club was only a few blocks away and grabbing Ibrahim's

sleeve, she dragged him along the street with her as she broke into a swift trot and headed towards the venue. In the dimly gas-lit club Jane spotted some of Alice's work mates who told her

"She said she felt a bit queasy and went into the ladies' toilet assisted by a woman who said she was a nurse. She looked Chinese."

Jane punched a number into her mobile and thrusting it into Ibrahim's hand, ordered him to tell the call receiver where they were and to redirect the armed back-up team. She knew she could not wait for their arrival and sprinted through a door and down a dark corridor. She ignored the closed for maintenance sign on the women's toilet door and kicked it open, drawing her powerful automatic as she burst in.

The sight that greeted her was both shocking and pitiful. Alice was stripped to her waist and tied to a water pipe. The skin of her right breast was still smoking from the scorching burns inflicted by a small, evil looking man who was holding a flaming blow-torch. Flanking the girl was a giant thug armed with a baseball bat and the Chinese nurse brandishing a long and lethal looking knife, which had been used to cut long slashes down Alice's arms. The poor girl could no longer stand and wracked with sobs she slid down the pipe, slumping onto the floor in a pool of her own blood. Jane's double-tap shot took the torturer in the chest and between his disbelieving eyes. The roar of her gun was deafening and reverberated off the echo-chamber like walls. The deceased had dropped the still burning blow-torch which fell onto the foot of the tall bruiser, causing him to cry out and jump as the flame scorched his trousers. Jane seized on this distraction and wanting to keep him alive for questioning delivered a vicious kick to his groin with her steel-toed brogue and stabbed her knife through his hand, pinning it to the cubicle's door frame.

Ibrahim burst in and surveyed the scene of carnage with simultaneous feelings of horror and admiration for the chaos Kate had perpetrated and the revenge she had exacted on the torturer and his hapless bodyguard. But before he could speak he was roughly shouldered aside by the first of the armed officers who shouted a warning.

"Armed Police! Armed Police! Put down your weapons and put your hands in the air or we will shoot."

Jane complied readily and when the armed men had verified her identity she turned her attention to the wounded and traumatised girl who lay crying and sobbing on the floor. In the confusion that followed she had failed to locate the nurse, who had escaped from the premises, leaving no trace, apart from her abandoned knife, and no sign of where she might have gone.

Before the paramedics had put her painlessly to sleep, Alice told Jane that she had confessed to them that the base was in the Kimberley but she couldn't tell them precisely where. It was clear that although Jane had plugged the leak, the word had had already seeped out.

Confronted and turned

Ibrahim was taken to a safe house where he was subjected to ruthless and relentless interrogation by hardened and unsympathetic intelligence officers. His story rang true and checked out. He was distraught at what he had done and full of remorse. He had been imprisoned without trial and in his isolation cell he had plenty of time to worry about what might happen to his family on account of his failure and by what method he would be executed for spying during time of war.

9

Kopassus Landing

In a strange land

The landing of the Kopassus commando unit from a Chinese nuclear sub went without a hitch. The velvet-dark tropical night concealed their arrival and the fast incoming tide soon erased the signs of their landing on a lonely beach somewhere on Australia's unguarded northern shore. Abdul breathed in the moist, warm sea air, relieved at escaping from the confines of the submarine and marvelled at the silence and lack of people along this vast stretch of coast. There was plenty of room here for the people from overcrowded Javanese fishing communities to start a healthier and more prosperous life, he thought, but then his Sergeant's terse report dispelled this indulgent reverie.

"All the men safely ashore and accounted for sir!"

"Thank you, Sergeant, get them off the beach as quickly as you can and ensure we leave no trace of our arrival."

It seemed strange to be landing on foot when they were used to airborne insertion or at least landing with jet-powered hover craft to carry them rapidly across any sort of terrain. But, his orders had stressed the need for their landing to be undetected and despite the crippling of Australia's surveillance satellites, the use of mechanised transport was an unacceptable risk.

The unit set off in single file, swinging into a steady, relentless gait, despite the considerable burden of their equipment and weapons. The precise location of their target was still unknown but Abdul had been instructed to head into the heart of the Kimberley country under whose rocky strata the base must be hidden. The long hike would test their endurance, hard-earned by pitiless hikes across Chinese desert country and they would only travel by night, to cope with the tropical heat and reduce the risk of detection.

It was a strange land. Though lacking the lush jungle of his homeland, the steamy heat was just as draining and the mosquitos felt worse. Beyond the thin belt of tree cover they were confronted by vast plains of head-high grasses, richly watered by monsoon rains. It provided good hiding but made for hard going on foot, denied Abdul a clear view of the way ahead and was ideal for concealing the threat of ambush.

Ancestral feeling

Even on operational duty, Abdul still observed his obligation to pray and though this country seemed so alien to him he began to sense a spiritual presence which he hoped was Allah's beneficial protection.

"This seems such an empty god forsaken place Sergeant but I can't help thinking that we might share a common ancestry with the first people who came to settle here."

"Can't say I have ever thought about it sir, but are you suggesting we are connected with those primitive nomads who barely managed to live off this harsh land?"

"I'm certainly not equating their godless culture with ours but there could be an ancient genetic link. But I must confess, mad as it might seem to you, the very stillness and silence of this country gives me a feeling of a brooding, hidden presence that is watching us."

"Careful Captain, too much thinking can be dangerous on this kind of assignment. Remember the men who became delirious in the desert and swore they could see an oasis ahead when there was nothing but sand. Isolation and loneliness can do that to you. But I get your drift and I must confess the men seem keener than usual to get their prayer mats out."

A helping hand

But they were not alone and help was at hand. Though denied communication with their commanders the Chinese had successfully infiltrated agents into the north and it was a relief to enter the brightly fire-lit cave where, as planned, they were greeted by a cheerful, little man offering welcome cups of warm and refreshing tea.

Mike Chang was no newcomer to Australia. His ancestors had arrived in Victoria during the nineteenth century gold-rush and then moved north and across from Queensland on cattle drives with the pioneer pastoralists, acting as cooks and gardeners at the stations established across the Kimberley. His speech was pure strine and everything about him was true blue dinky-di. But his grandfather had enthralled him with stories of China's ancient Imperial glory, advanced technical achievements and rich culture. Like most of the Chinese diaspora embedded in developed western societies, he had maintained his affection for the motherland and nurtured a wistful longing that one day the Dragon would rise again. With the new China's economic and military renaissance his wish had been fulfilled and he had welcomed the call to help support its super-power ambitions.

"Welcome to the Kimberley Captain. I'm afraid this is not as comfortable and the tucker not a patch on a Chinese restaurant but then I'm no Chinese waiter and things can get a lot rougher up here."

"We are glad to have found you Mr Chang. Your fire and food are very welcome and we need all the help you can give us."

"Skip the formality cap, after all this is Australia and my name is Mike."

"Ok Mike. What can you tell me about this place?"

Mike was certainly no Chinese waiter. In every part of him, apart from his face, he would pass at any cattle muster as a born and bred Australian bushman or stockman. His moleskin pants and RM Williams boots bore the stains and scars of hard outdoor wear and his thick denim shirt was bleached almost colourless from too much time in the sun. His battered and wide brimmed bush-hat completed the picture of a regular Kimberley roustabout.

"I don't know where the base is but I can give you some tips to help you on your way. It's most likely somewhere in or near the Purnalulu national park-once known as the Bungle Bungles, because the rocky ranges would provide the ideal concealment for such a facility. But that is a big inhospitable place and you will still have to do some searching to find it. There is one major river to cross on the way which is too dangerous to tackle in the wet without boats but as the monsoon season is over you should be able to float across with care.

There are bugger all people around but be alert to Aboriginal hunting parties. They won't attack you but they could dob you in with the army and as you'll expect those Norforce bastards are prowling about and you certainly don't want to tangle with them. There are fish in the river, Kangaroos are easy to kill but, of course, shots will give you away and it may be best to butcher one of the wild buffalo you will meet on the track, but watch for their horns, they can be deadly. Maps are not much use here but I can give you the necessary compass bearings to your search zone. All the snakes can kill you so try to avoid them. Otherwise, that's about all I can do for you."

"What about communications, can you help us get messages out?"

"That's not easy but, if absolutely necessary, I have some Aboriginal connections and could get one of them to run out with a written message. But electronic contacts are impossible. They would attract a missile strike as soon as you went on air."

"Well thanks for that and if I can get some more of that wallaby stew I'll get some sleep and be ready to move out at nightfall."

Watchers awake

It was true there were few people in that wilderness but to the hunter coming back with a haul of Kangaroo meat, this was his home, where he lived off its bounty and travelled the land with such certainty and ease that every trail might have been signposted. He didn't see the fire in the cave but the sweet smell of stewing meat reminded him of his hunger and alerted him to the presence of other travellers in his country.

His native caution prevented his approaching the source of the delicious aroma but without having the confirmation of a visual sighting he knew that whoever was in the cave was not one of his people as they would never cook their food using such alien spices.

Back at his camp, he told the elders what he had discovered and although they couldn't fathom its meaning they had been strongly counselled by passing Norforce scouts to pass on such information, immediately, and that as well as doing their duty they would be rewarded for their help.

10

Spies in the North

Ibrahim heard the heavy rhythmic tread of marching feet before their owners reached the door of his cell. He braced himself for at least another tough interrogation session and he feared their frustration with what little he had been able to tell them would lead to more painful methods.

To his surprise and relief the prison officers who opened his cell's door were more than civil in asking him to accompany them to the meeting room where visitors were waiting for him. But, instead of stopping and leaving him at the visitors centre, they escorted him up a flight of steps through what appeared to be an administrative area and into an office where he was told to take a seat in a softly upholstered arm chair.

At a glance he took in the shelves of books, the large desk, olive green velvet drapes, keeping out the night-time chill and the inviting glow of a log fire in an elaborate open fireplace. His glance was necessarily brief as his sense of smell made an overwhelming claim on his sensory priorities. A small table, before the fire, contained plates of enticing pastries and gourmet sandwiches. But what really grabbed his attention was the enticing aroma of fresh brewed coffee.

After days of prison fare this was a gift from the gods. But before he could help himself two people entered the room sat in the other two chairs beside the food table and directly opposite him. He was delighted to see Jane again but he was unsure and apprehensive about the intentions of the tall, well-built man in military uniform who accompanied her. Jane gave him a fleeting smile of recognition but the man spoke first.

"Ibrahim, you can see from my uniform that I am a soldier. My name is of no relevance to you but you should know that I am a senior officer in Military Intelligence and Miss Smith reports to me. I don't know whether you appreciate what a serious predicament you are in and it is my first duty to make this absolutely clear to you. During wartime, and we are at war, the penalty for spying on behalf of the enemy is death. Your being an Australian citizen compounds your crime and makes it more likely you will face execution. Have you anything to say for yourself?"

Although Ibrahim anticipated this confirmation that he might die, he felt an in-voluntary leak from his bladder seep into his trousers and his hands and voice began to tremble.

"I know that what I have done is a betrayal of this, my new country and this fills me with the deepest shame. I have expected that you would kill me and I can offer no defence that would disprove my guilt."

The act of speaking steadied him a little and prevented his breaking down. He knew that slow, deep breathing helped calm frayed nerves and as the ensuing silence continued without either Jane or her boss breaking it, a small glimmer of hope entered his gloomy mind and began to grow. He would not be in this comfortable place faced with the possibility of a good wholesome feed if they intended to hang him. Clearly, they wanted something from him and he realised that he must bargain for his life.

"I can at least offer some explanation for my treachery. It is true that as a citizen with dual and now conflicting nationalities I still feel loyalty to the land of my birth and sympathise with the fix it is in as a result of China's aggression towards Russia. But I would not have committed this act of betrayal except for the threat to the lives of my family in Indonesia. With this in mind, I acknowledge my guilt and throw myself upon your mercy." With this, he averted his gaze, lowered his head into his hands and began to sob uncontrollably.

Jane suppressed her innate feelings of sympathy and gripped the arms of her chair to prevent herself crossing the room to comfort him. Her colleague showed no sign of caring for Ibrahim but when he spoke he was quick to suggest that Ibrahim might be able to escape the gallows.

"Despite our understanding of your motivation for betraying us, if there were no way in which you might redeem yourself by helping us, your execution would be assured. However there is a way in which you can be of value to us and that is by becoming a double agent. If you agree to this proposal you will enjoy a stay of execution and we will develop and leak a story which will prove to your Indonesian controller that not only did you tell us nothing but also that you persuaded us of your innocence."

At this proposal a wave of relief flooded trough Ibrahim's mind and body and with a quavering voice he accepted and assured them that, "I am grateful for this second chance and I will do anything to help you and restore my honour. But whilst I am unconcerned for my safety I still fear for my family and need your assurance that you will do all that you can to protect them and perhaps find a way to bring them to safety here in Australia."

Both listeners nodded their assent and Jane gave Ibrahim's hand a reassuring squeeze and handed him a box of tissues while her boss poured him a mug of strong black coffee.

Double agent

Embedded Chinese agents picked up the carefully orchestrated story that Australian Military Intelligence leaked in support of Ibrahim's alibi and swallowed it hook line and sinker. They still put him through a vigorous series of interrogations but they were unable to find any cracks in his explanation of why the enemy had released him and they were loath to lose such a useful agent in place.

Although he did not know the precise location of the base, he would be useful in using his technical skills and experience to assess the likelihood of any location proposed by the infiltration force being a viable site for its communication purposes. They had no intention of sending him into the field where he would be an impediment to the team's progress but he was ordered to find a reason for basing himself in Broome where Chinese agents could consult with him about the options the Kopassus force deemed worth consideration.

Within days of Ibrahim's report on the instructions from his Chinese handlers, he and Jane were flying north on the pretext that he had been assigned to review the effectiveness of telecommunication resources in that north-west city.

Clubbing in Broome

Jane and Ibrahim started their search for enemy spies by joining social clubs and attending dance nights. The massive pre-war expansion of food and energy trade with Asia had sparked such growth in population and infrastructure that large social clubs had sprung up to cater for the relaxation needs of men and women working in the energy and agriculture industries and the substantial military forces that defended them.

The Food Bowl Club was the favourite stamping ground of Asian agronomists and food processing experts who had migrated and settled to make the Kimberley food bowl expansion possible. This was the obvious place to throw out their first trawl. Ibrahim's Indonesian nationality and good looks ensured a warm welcome on their first dance night.

Having selected their buffet dinners, they approached the dining tables and were urged to join one occupied by Chinese and Vietnamese families. Well educated Indians kept to themselves and Philippinos maintained a Christian only diaspora along with

East Timorese. When the dancing started they divided their forces by taking the floor with different partners and whilst they had a good time and learned a lot about multicultural Broome, no information or contacts relevant to their search eventuated.

After several equally fruitless contacts they had decided to leave when a cheerful Chinese waiter complimented them on their taste for Chinese food and recommended they try Man Fang, a very up market restaurant in Broome's largest casino where the food was cooked by gold medal winning chefs from China's epicurean regions. As they left the club Jane asked Ibrahim why he seemed so pleased by that recommendation.

"Because that is where my Chinese controllers have told me to meet with their local agent."

Laying false trails

Ibrahim obeyed his instructions and visited Man Fang without Jane on the following afternoon. He gave his waiter the prescribed order and soon after he had disappeared into the kitchen an elegantly dressed manager emerged and invited Ibrahim to join him in a back office. He was greeted by a prosperous looking Chinese man who got right to the point.

"In anticipation of your finding the precise location of the Kimberley communication base a squadron of Indonesian Kopassus special-forces will land on the Australian coast and move inland to destroy it. It is vital that their arrival is kept secret for as long as possible and you will give your military intelligence contacts false information to lead them off the track."

Ibrahim made the unspoken inference that this was also a further check on his reliability as an agent for the Chinese underground.

Within hours of his reporting back to Jane, an Australian navy patrol boat slipped out of Darwin harbour to take up station off the north-west Kimberley coast and commence its fruitless search for enemy infiltrators who had already landed in a different location, undetected by coastal surveillance and unknown to Ibrahim.

Having passed this further test Ibrahim was entrusted with the identity of a Chinese field agent who would help the Kopassus force and his informant, whose name was Chang, also confided that this man was his cousin.

11

Kimberley Commander

Taking charge

Frank Bevan was about to board the return flight taking him back to his posting down south, when a military messenger caught-up with him and handed him an order to return at once to Norforce Command Headquarters in Broome. The Commander's greeting was warm and effusive.

"Welcome back Major Bevan."

"Didn't expect to see you again so soon, sir and by the way, it's Captain Bevan."

"Not any longer young man. Your promotion will be well earned and is effective immediately. You will understand why when you hear your orders. You have been reassigned to Norforce and will take command of the forces in the Kimberley region. Your predecessor who led that impressive ambush busted his back in a training accident and Army Command has insisted that you replace him."

"Please don't think me ungrateful for the instant promotion sir but, with respect, I have done a stint out there and to return, even with an elevated rank, might be construed as something of a backward career step."

"If I were to tell you that we have detected a Kopassus patrol on the loose in the Kimberley, searching for our communication base, and that you have been tasked to lead the forces that will find and kill them, might this ease your disappointment at this re-assignment?"

"Too bloody right it does, sir. When do I go and who will I have to help me do the job?"

"That's more like it. In the next room you will find a Sergeant-Major, who may be known to you, who has your combat kit and your preferred choice of weapons. You will receive a full briefing from me at 0900 Hours and make sure you get a hearty breakfast before that because from then on you will be living on field rations and water recycled from your combat suit."

Frank saluted smartly and ran to get his kit.

"G'day Major congratulations on your promotion and may I say what a pleasure it will be serving with you again, sir."

"Higgins, you old Bastard, what have I done to have to serve with you again. Thought I had seen the last of you when I left the SAS at Swanbourne."

"Well sir, as you are so rusty at doing real soldiering again, the top brass thought you needed your trusty nurse-maid with you and as you only have these weekend warriors to command I am here to provide some SAS stiffening".

With that exchange completed they shook hands heartily and Frank grabbed his gear and followed the tantalising aroma of grilled bacon towards the mess. Later, when checking the contents of his pack, he found a note from Higgins regretting the absence of celebratory champagne and suggesting that the half-bottle of Laphroaig single malt whisky secreted in a side pocket might make the recycled water more potable.

Orders to kill

The briefing was short and to the point. An unknown number of Kopassus commandos had been located on the ground in the Kimberley, having arrived undetected presumably from an enemy submarine. Frank would be heading up a Norforce unit tasked to find them and if necessary kill every one of them before they could do any damage to the communications base. Frank and his men would be transported overland under cover of darkness to the edge of the Purnalulu Park. It was deemed unsafe to fly them in as the Chinese might still be able to track and shoot down any airborne transport.

Lest we forget

He took full advantage of the few hours remaining before jump-off time to make a lightening visit to the family Cattle station. Frank had come to pay his respects and say goodbye not to his parents, who had moved to Perth leaving it in charge of a manger, but to two of his revered ancestors whose graves stood sheltered by a grove of peppercorn trees, close to the homestead.

Although they had died decades earlier, so long ago that Frank had never even met them, his father had told him their story so often that he felt that he really knew them and he could even converse with them at their graves sides as though they were really still alive. As a boy he had thrilled to the accounts of Dan Bevan's heroism during the First World War and of how he had come to Australia, defied IRA assassins and built up the Kimberley Cattle station, on which the Bevan family's prosperity still depended. Dan's wife Liza was celebrated. She had driven ambulances behind the Western Front in France, fought with the suffragettes to get women the vote and it was she that had shot the gunman, who was threatening Dan's life.

Even more impressive was Dan's re-enlisting with the Nackeroos, the forerunners of Norforce, during the Second World War to beat off Japanese invaders in the Kimberley. At that time he was no spring chicken and now that Frank was to take on a similar challenge in his early forties, he felt a great affinity with the elder Bevan hoping fervently that he would be as determined, brave and stoical as Dan had proved to be when the going got very tough.

Dedication to the cause

"Hi Dan and Liza. Lying here, you must be amazed at seeing history repeating itself. I am sure you are gobsmacked by the politicians allowing this to happen all over again and wondering that another Bevan has drawn the short straw of having to defend the north once more. When I think of what you did, Dan, at your age, I am both humbled and proud to be following in your footsteps.

I promise not to let you down and I will do my damnedest to defeat the invaders even if I lose my life in doing it. I am unmarried Liza and so have nobody close to mourn me if the worst happens but in a strange way I am comforted by the knowledge that should I not return alive, at least, I will come to be with you both for ever, under the shade of these trees, in this lovely corner of our country. I must go now. I will never forget you and always take pride in what you did. In return, I hope you will have cause to be equally proud of me."

Brushing tears from his cheeks, Frank stood at attention for a further, fleeting moment before racing away to catch his transport back to the Norforce base. His mind was in a whirl with the conflicting emotions of pride in remembrance, a warrior's lust for battle and more than a touch of fear. He recalled that Dan had been born and raised in Manchester where it was said he had developed his rock-hard determination never to give in. Some called this native stubbornness and he dearly hoped that some of this indomitable courage and talent for survival had been passed on to himself as part of his ancestral Mancunian DNA.

Unleashing the hounds from hell

Back at the base, his troops were loading their kit onto the hover transports ready for the off. There was just time for him to gather them around him in a half circle and say a few words of encouragement and reassurance before they went to risk their lives for each other and for their country . All of his men were volunteers who served for much more than their modest pay and brought their own motivation with them. He was not big on Shakespearean style speeches before going into action, nor was he a devotee of the football coach's inspirational rant. He spoke to them in a quiet but firm tone using language they would understand and accept.

"Alright men. We are facing a very difficult and dangerous task but it is one that is vital to the future security of our nation and many others beyond our shores. I have served with the regiment before. I know what you can do and I have every confidence in your doing your job, supporting your mates and coming safe home. I have been away from active duty for some time and will necessarily be a bit rusty and not as fit as I should be, so I will need your fullest cooperation and total support.

But I assure you of my commitment to our common cause. My experience from several active tours of duty with the SAS will come to the fore, especially if and when things get rough and we are joined and strengthened by the addition of Sergeant-Major Higgins whose combat record and decorations for bravery under fire are well known to you.

Finally, be wary of our enemy. We will be up against crack Kopassus troops. I trained some of them on joint exercises with our SAS and we need to respect their professionalism and toughness. They will be well armed and will give no quarter so, subject to our usual rules of engagement, if they will not surrender, we will kill them and we will not allow any of us to be taken alive by them. Is that clear?

They will be aware of our reputation too-they call us the hounds from hell-and they will be every bit as wary, maybe even more afraid of us than we are of them and we have them on our ground.

This is the last chance for questions before we board our transport and go into silent operational mode. Are there any questions? No? Well let's go."

River of no return

Mike had been right about the river. It would still be a challenge to cross it now but the evidence of mounds of scree and discarded boulders along its banks testified to its power and lethal force when it had been in full-spate.

Their crossing technique was well practised and the men needed no orders from Abdul or his Sergeant to lay down their packs, lash them together to form a raft and to stretch condoms over their guns to protect them from the river water. Circling the pack-raft and securing hand holds the troops pushed off into the racing river aiming to swim diagonally across the surging water to land a little further down-stream on the opposite bank.

They were more than half way across when the water on one side of the raft exploded in a violent maelstrom, throwing spay over all the swimmers. A terrible scream shattered the silence and the raft lurched to one side before continuing its unbalanced drift to the safety of the bank. Quickly, they broke up the raft, each claiming his own pack and only realising when one lay on the ground, unclaimed, that a man was missing.

Looking back across the unbroken surface of the racing river, Abdul could see no sign of the man who had become separated from the raft and presumably swept away. An immediate search of the tangle of tree roots and reeds along the bank found no sign of the lost soldier and it was presumed that he had been drowned until the Sergeant called out and held up a large sign which had been cut down and discarded in the undergrowth. Its words of warning sent shivers of fear down Abdul's spine and his men cried out in horror. Dangerous crocodiles inhabit this area. Attacks cause injury or death.

Mike had told them the river crossing could be tricky but he had neglected to mention the crocs.

12

Death of an Elder

By the spirit pool

Drawn by the sickly-sweet smell, they found the dead men against a rock overhang close by the sacred pool, looked down on in death by the unwavering guardian-gaze of their ancestral Wandjina, whose wall painting the elder and his team of tribal kinsmen had come to restore at the end of the wet season, in accordance with their traditional duty. For all but their leader, death had been brutal and sudden. There was plentiful evidence of the indiscriminate use of machete and bayonet to despatch the defenceless men, in preference to using scarce ammunition and to maintain a deadly silence.

Frank looked down on their leader's barely distinguishable face and his skin, like tan bark, smoked, crisped and charcoaled by the fire over which he had been slowly roasted alive, to loosen his tongue. This torture was a known hallmark of Kopassus troops and in the long ago Konfrontasi between Indonesia and Malaysia, captured Australian and British SAS troopers had suffered the same fate. But now he had seen its results with his own eyes and nothing in his previous experience had sickened and grieved him like this pitiful sight.

There could be no doubting who the perpetrators had been. He did not know where they had gone nor whether, as a result of this dastardly deed, they had found out where to go. Whilst he could not accept this bestiality and elimination of innocent witnesses to their passing, deployment and direction, he understood their ruthless commitment to their task. But to conduct such inhuman torture told of darker forces than military necessity and he and his men resolved to exact the fullest retribution. His aboriginal comrades were sure that the power of the vengeful Wandjina would ensure the spirits of these butchers would never leave this land.

The Wandjina calls

The late shift at Bungle Bungle base had ended and as Kate settled into the first level of soporific sleep, the dreams came in. She had been inducted into her father's dreaming, which was no longer forbidden to women, because of the increasing shortage of suitably prepared men and as the influence of sexual equality from external society had overwhelmed the ancient tribal codes. She understood and shared her tribe's obligation to preserve the painting of their Wandjina spirit on the Kimberley rock wall and despite her scientific scepticism, she was able to accept her father's claim to have dream connection with the spirit world.

But the images that now confronted her seemed real and as tangible as a cinema programme screening in her head. "What was going on?" she wondered and as the scene came into clearer focus, she could see soldiers killing unarmed men near a sacred site. "Oh God!" she gasped, it was her father and his restoration team being attacked. Suddenly she jerked awake, blasted from the dream by the realisation that, through the power of the Wandjina, her father had transferred these dreams to her mind to tell her that he was dead.

Sick at heart and trembling with the shock of this revelation, Kate turned to the spirit world for solace and direction. For a long time nothing happened and then as her breathing became so slow and measured as to almost threaten her life, out of the darkness emerged the mournful, mystical face of the Wandjina, projected onto the wall of her room. Its lustrous sorrowful eyes now burned with the intensity of twin lasers, searing its message into Kate's subconscious mind.

She asked the spirit for direction. At first there was no response then, as her breathing quickened, close by the Wandjina's head there appeared the figure of a soldier wearing a red beret. She was stunned-this was the primordial ritual process for directing the spirit's destructive power onto its victim and which inevitably led to a painful and lingering death. When she was fully awake, she stretched and tried to take all this in. She had heard of people dying as a result of such curses but never of this being initiated by the spirit itself. The foul deed had summoned up unprecedented forces deeply embedded in the foundation of the land. Then with a convulsive shudder and a cry she knew that she rather than the Wandjina was to be the agent of revenge and the agent of death.

As the night deepened, the opposing forces of Frank and Abdul converged on the satellite base; one intent on its destruction the other determined to destroy the would-be attackers, whilst Kate set out to call her tribal relations together and order ritual preparations for the killing to begin.

13

Hot Pursuit

Kimberley heat

High on the treeless escarpment the tropical sun struck like a hammer blow, super-heating the sluggish air to better than forty degrees. Rivulets of sweat streamed down Frank's body making his sodden combat smock cling like a surfer's wet-suit. Slowly, through the filter of his compressed and cracking lips, he sucked in scorching air to relieve his straining lungs as he and his patrol trudged up a steep incline in the full glare of the merciless afternoon sun. It was a bad day to be going out to kill.

Shards of rock cut into the soles of his boots, causing him to stumble and sway under the dead-weight of his pack, loaded with spare ammo and his personal weapons, as the track narrowed to a knife-edge. It was the wrong time of day and year to be slogging across a Kimberley range on a mission whose success could only be measured in numbers of enemy dead. Although his combat suit captured his perspiration and recycled and purified this along with his urine, ensuring a constant source of drinking water, it never seemed enough and not even the thought of enjoying last night's beer again, lessened his nagging thirst.

The heat and terrain would have more than tested the most combat-hardened veteran but at his age and moderate degree of fitness, Frank struggled to match the pace of his younger and fitter men. As an SAS officer he had survived the rigours of Arctic warfare training and jungle fighting, which had claimed the lives of many close friends. But that was long ago and the strength and fitness of those days was more easily remembered than relived.

He had signed-on as a part-time member of Norforce to offset the routine of running a remote gas processing plant and to indulge his love of the timeless Kimberley wilderness. But the wartime recall to duty had not prepared him for what was no routine exercise and his and his men's lives would depend on how well he could rediscover his combat and leadership skills.

Contact

As Frank's patrol descended into the welcome cool of a gorge riddled with enticing caves and shady rock overhangs, they were spooked by an eruption of fruit bats piercing the intense silence with their shrill squeaks and tainting the air with their noisome odour. Though light on combat experience the patrol had been rigorously trained and their Aboriginal members knew what this foretold and reacted instinctively in taking up defensive positions against the cause of this noisy incursion and the threat it implied. They blessed the relentless training by their instructors and their bush heritage when the trail ahead of them erupted as though thrust up by an earth tremor and a savage hail of steel splines shredded the topmost fronds of the canyon's sheltering palms, ricocheting from rock to rock face in search of softer human targets.

Blinded by billowing smoke and dust, Frank was slow to recover from his temporary deafness and the hammering reverberations of the blast inside his head. But the style of this ambush was no surprise as the combination of land mines under the trail and more strung up in the trees, connected to trip wires above and close to the ground, was a favourite SAS tactic which Kopassus had learned and adopted after conducting joint training exercises with their Australian counterparts. He would say no more unkind words about fruit bats whose timely alarm had warned of the enemy's presence and whose panicked flight had triggered the snares intended for weary and unwary pursuers.

Tried and proven weapons, no matter how old, could still kill but Frank was quick to repay his enemy's enterprise with a newer and equally deadly reply. A 'Switchblade' backpack drone tore off its launcher, shooting up to hover above the assumed enemy location, whilst its operator scanned the target area through its video camera to get a fix on his prey. Abdul knew what was coming and had urged his men to cling to the canyon walls and take cover under rocky overhangs. Although their training had been in arid conditions in China and they understood the need to tread lightly and obscure their trail marks, due to their lack of bush craft they had failed to keep to rocky ground and despite their precautions, the heavily laden soldiers had left detectable foot prints in a few patches of soft sand. The Switchblade operator could not see the men, but he saw their tracks and knowing exactly where they were sheltering released its deadly missile straight down onto a narrow rock overhang under which the Kopassus men were concealed.

The direct hit failed to find a human target but the powerful warhead brought down the whole rock-face with a mighty crash. Judging by the screams that followed some damage had been done and when they judged it safe to advance Frank's forward scout found a dead Indonesian soldier, who had been crushed by the rock-fall and a blood trail suggested that the rest were encumbered with a wounded comrade.

14

Strike Back

Tribe at war

The men of Kate's tribe were in shock and mad as hell at the death of their brothers and the brutal torture and slaying of their tribal leader. The defiling of the sacred site, beside the spirit pool and under the gaze of their Wandjina, compounded their grief and intensified their anger.

Her reception by the men had been better than she had expected and her installation had been hurried and devoid of great ceremony because of their impatience at waiting to get after the perpetrators and exact terrible revenge on them. The young and active tribesmen milled around hopelessly. After hundreds of years of peace they were at a loss as to how they should prepare for and go to war. It was not until an old greybeard, who could hardly walk, was helped from his bed and consulted about the appropriate tribal traditions and ceremonies that they were finally able to vent their spleen and whip up their blood lust by joining in the required weapons dances which announced their preparation for battle.

Head to head

Military commanders had pieced together news of the Kopassus incursion, their murder of Kate's father and Jane's location of Chinese agents based in Broome. To ensure that the three elements in the field did not compromise their separate actions Frank, Kate and Jane were ordered to pool their information and coordinate their plans of action via Thought Mail.

All three had undergone the procedure to place Thought Mail nodes into their heads and had a brief familiarisation session before going into action. Frank was amazed at the speed and clarity of the communication but at first it was a bit disconcerting to have to distinguish a message from his own natural thought process. After a brief identification and re-introduction they got down to business. As Frank was the ranking officer and closest to the enemy it was agreed that he should coordinate the exchange.

"G'day Kate and Jane welcome to the Kimberley. I hope to meet you in person soon or when this is over. The situation here is that we have made contact with the Indons and inflicted some damage but they are moving on in search of the communication base. They have attempted to ambush us and it is clear they are very alert and dangerous. Over to you Jane."

"Hi Frank, glad to hear you are still safe and in pursuit. We have established that a Chinese Australian from Broome has been helping the Kopassus force. He is very familiar with the Kimberley and as good a bushman as you would find in these parts. If it would be helpful to you, we are able to pass messages to him via his Broome masters and we would be glad to feed him some misinformation."

"Thanks Jane that could be very useful. Good to have you on our side. Kate, I am truly, truly sorry about the death of your father and his companions. Rest assured that their bodies were treated with appropriate respect by my men and they are being conveyed back to you by local tribesmen."

"Thank you Frank, it is a comfort to know they are in the care of our people. As you will appreciate our men are mad as hell and it has taken all of my newfound authority as head of the tribe to restrain them from a direct attack on the killers."

"Yes I can understand that but kate, promise me you will do

all that you can to hold them back and at least limit their actions to observation and sabotage, if necessary. The Kopassus troops are very experienced and ruthless as they demonstrated in killing your kin. I don't want you to lose any more of your people and it is imperative that they don't get caught in the cross-fire of our attacks. I will try to give warning of what we intend to do but understand that situations may compel us to take action without notice."

"Understood Frank, but easier said than done when their blood is up. But I will do my best to keep them to the role you have outlined."

"Thanks to both of you. Be ready to receive further reports from me at all times. Perhaps Jane, it may be possible to use some misinformation to slow them down and reel in their helper at the same time. Kate's hunters could find and take him out and that might hold them back from dangerous headstrong action. Over and out."

Hard lessons

Regardless of Kate's warning and best effort to restrain the young men, they rushed away and sought to trap the invaders in a rocky defile. Their plan was good and they were well concealed but they had not allowed sufficiently for the Indonesian's technology.

A silent, low flying back-pack drone had scattered sensors on the track ahead of the ground party and their heat sensors picked up the presence of the waiting attackers. It was only the bush skills of the aboriginal warriors that enabled them to disengage and sneak away with the loss of only one man and minor wounds suffered by two others. Jane was both angry and concerned when they returned bearing their dead comrade and supporting the wounded. But at the same time she was glad the lesson had not been worse and that it would at least reinforce her authority.

Locking the gate

Frank's brush with the Kopassus force had confirmed their presence and their approximate location. Military command was quick to call in the standby ready-reaction infantry force from Darwin and deploy them around the Bungle Bungle base rendering it impregnable to all but a massive force attack or inconceivable sabotage by an insider.

This locked the gate and neutralised the enemy's destruction goal. But it failed to remove the pressure from Frank's Norforce team to search them out and destroy them. This seemed to be a straight forward mopping up task until a message came in from Kate.

"Frank, after the failure of our attempted ambush of the visitors I sent out stalking patrols to keep them under observation but I am afraid that after receiving reports from all of them that the Indonesians are nowhere in sight, I must confess that we have lost them."

"Kate, how can that be? Your trackers are the best in the business and the Bungle Bungles are their own back yard."

"This is very embarrassing and puzzling Frank. I can only surmise that they are receiving some form of local help to become as invisible as this. Our guys were blocked from searching beyond our land by the neighbouring tribe with which we have had strained relations for many years and this has raised our suspicions. We will keep looking but perhaps it is time to get Jane to send out a message via her contact in the enemy camp and hope that this might smoke them out."

"Yes, you are right. I will consult my commander and Jane's boss to see what might best achieve that result. In the meanwhile suggest you consult your elders about possible hiding places and consider whether there might be any Chinese sympathisers amongst other local tribes."

Broome for orders

Wherever the Kopassus element was holed up, they could go nowhere without being detected by Kate's watchers who picketed the rival tribe's territory. Frank was ordered to rely on the locals to maintain the watch and he and his patrol were ordered back to Broome to confer and review strategy.

An intelligence analyst at the command meeting summarised the current situation.

"The Indons have suffered injury and probably a fatality as a result of Norforce action and they have gone into hiding with the help of their field agent and disaffected locals who believe they will get a better deal should the Chinese prevail. Our main ready reaction force has surrounded the Bungle Bungle base and there is no way the enemy force can breach this cordon to attack it."

"So, what are our options Lieutenant?"

"We have two main challenges, General. Despite their no longer being a threat to the base we will need to search out and destroy the Kopassus force. They are not emitting any electronic signals and so we need to step up searches by friendly locals to find them so that Norforce can finish them off. At the same time, after we have used our man to feed them false information about our intentions, we must roll-up the Chinese fifth column based in Broome to cut off Kopassus from all external contact and help."

"Let's tackle them in priority order. Jane and Frank need to confer about the sort of mis-information that would be likely to lure the enemy out of hiding. Norforce will then move in to capture or eliminate them. At the same time Jane and her Military Intelligence colleagues will move in on the local spies. Unless you have anything else to add I suggest you proceed with all speed to bring these operations to a swift and satisfactory end."

Frank meets Jane

"G'day Jane, good to meet you in person."

"You too Frank. You did a good job of putting a spoke in Kopassus' wheel."

"Not good enough though as they were able to escape and go to ground before we could do some real damage. We need to smoke them out, what do you think might bring them into the open?"

"I'm not sure but by now they would be aware that the base is heavily defended. We need to make them believe there is still a way they can cripple the base without launching a frontal attack. By the way, I must get a signal to kate not to pick up Mike Chang until we have used him to lead them astray."

"The base commander would have some plausible suggestions about taking the base off-line that we could feed to them. I will get in touch with him and until then I haven't had a decent feed since before we went bush perhaps you would like to join me for dinner?"

"That would be good as long as we eat anything other than Chinese and certainly steer clear of the Man Fang."

Combining to serve

The prime rib, washed down with a robust Shiraz at the Combined Forces Club, tasted really sweet to Frank after existing for days on field rations and recycled water. Jane had gone for a more delicate but no less rewarding sea-food platter.

"So what's your story Frank? You must be highly thought of to be given such a free hand in leading the Norforce operation."

"More a case of being in the right or wrong place at the time, depending on one's viewpoint and how well or badly things turn out."

"What brought you to that position?"

"I used to be an SAS regular and although I have been a

gas plant engineer in civvy-street for a long time now, I joined Norforce as a reserve officer just to keep my hand in and to get to know more of the fabulous Kimberley country. When the war began I was drafted back in and happened to be on the spot when the usual Norforce commander was knocked out by an accidental injury."

"How about you Jane? If you will forgive me saying so yours is a mighty tough job for a woman."

"You're not wrong Frank, but I was not brought up as a shrinking violet. Captain of hockey at school and at university. I even tried women's rugby and Aussie rules footy. So when my Asian studies background and language skills brought me to government attention it was no great hardship to join the military as a way of serving in Asian locations. The things I was involved in made me grow up fast and to harden both my body and heart against the usual feminine sensitivities. I guess like you I have even learned how to kill people and cope with the emotional fallout. You attached or single?"

"Married twice to lovely women but the restless searcher in me would not allow me to settle down sufficiently to meet their needs and so I have a few female friends but no serious attachment and I have grown comfortable with my own company. I come from a cattle station background and started young as a boundary rider in some very lonely places. How about you?"

"Often kissed but never married. The secret nature of my work and long time spent undercover in foreign parts has not allowed me to develop any serious partnerships. At the same time what the job has made of me is often a problem for most men who shy away when I reveal my hard, independent side. I can't ever see myself getting married and settling down, even when I leave this line of work but, at times I would like to have a special man out there who accepts me as I am and knows how to care for me without trying to take charge or wrap me in domestic bliss."

"Sounds like we have a similar take on life and relationships."

"Yes it does. Have you thought about what you will do when the war is over?"

"Being out patrolling in the bush gives you time to think and dream about how your life might be. After this bit of soldiering, I couldn't go back to engineering and it is likely I will return to the family property and take up some managerial responsibility. I am passionately in love with the Kimberley and I feel that it will have the power to heal any demons I bring back from this experience."

"That sounds wonderful. My father is a surgeon and so there is no family career succession waiting for me. I envy you your choice and I am at a loss to know what I will turn to next if I get through this in one piece."

Frank detected the rising emotion and regret in Jane's voice and before the conversation could become too maudlin he rose and invited her to dance. On the floor they realised that both had natural rhythm and the music led them into an easy slow foxtrot. At first they held each other at an appropriate degree of separation but after two circuits of the floor he felt her draw closer and nestle her cheek against his. The floor was crowded and the surrounding couples were all too content to focus on their own acts of intimacy and were oblivious of others. In response to Jane's tightening squeeze he nuzzled her cheek and gave it a peck. As they twirled he felt her leg slide between his and the thrust of her muscular thigh encouraged him to slide his hand down her back and squeeze her firm buttocks.

At the end of the number they agreed that it was time to go. She to her motel and he to the Norforce barracks. He thanked her for the evening and as she turned to slip into her taxi she drew back to kiss him, sliding her tongue between his teeth. He responded by slipping his hand into the gap between the buttons of her blouse, under her bra and whilst cupping her breast, teased her nipple between his thumb and finger. With a moan of arousal she disengaged from his embrace and with a knowing smile jumped into the cab which sped away

Before falling asleep Jane recalled that unplanned parting with a flush of pleasure and reflected on her feelings for Ibrahim, of whom she had become progressively fond and this new attraction to Frank. She had felt a twinge of carnal lust for Ibrahim when he had attempted to enter her and whilst there was still some physical magnetism for her, Frank was a much more complex and exciting prospect offering much more than just sexual delight. She anticipated with pleasure the recommencement of their working relationship tomorrow.

15

Counter Bluff

Salting the claim

Frank and Jane were cool and professional in their dealings with each other at their morning strategy meeting and the others present were given no hint of what had transpired between them the night before. Frank reported on his conversation with the base commander.

"He was very helpful and put forward a number of ideas of which one seemed to me the most believable option. The base relies on water from an underground aquifer for human consumption and for cooling of its equipment. If it were sabotaged, cutting off the supply, the base would become inoperable within 24 hours. Whilst this is true, there is a huge underground reserve of water in the base that is designed to meet such an emergency and which can keep the base on-line for weeks or until supply from the aquifer can be restored."

"That will do nicely." Jane responded with enthusiasm. "I will brief Ibrahim at once and we can embroider the story so that it will catch their instant attention."

"They will of course seek verification and as the commander believes that some of their cleaners and kitchen porters are members of the suspect tribe he will ensure that this aspect of the base's vulnerability will be discussed in places where they are likely to overhear and take note."

As the meeting broke up Jane trailed behind her colleagues and as she passed his desk, she reached out her hand and gently caressing Frank's fingers she gave him a meaningful wink. It was his turn to flush at the warm sensation radiating from his groin.

Ibrahim made his accustomed approach in contacting his minder at Man Fang and soon received confirmation that they were aware of the beefing up of the base's defences. He was careful to show no interest in the location of the Kopassus troops when, in response Chang's tabling of their dilemma, he tentatively suggested that there might be an alternative to attacking front on. His proposal was well received, although Chang made it clear that they would have to check the veracity of the information because they appreciated that the Australians were as adept as their British counterparts in creating credible subterfuges.

Ibrahim was commended and thanked profusely. His bank balance would be suitably enhanced in return for this valuable information that would salvage the mission and he was assured that the information would be relayed via Chang's cousin Mike to the saboteurs' commander, as soon as the aquifer's vital function had been confirmed.

Deep in the cave

Abdul and his men were relieved at being able to shelter from the harsh Kimberley sun. They were accustomed to warm humid conditions but the searing dry heat, boosted by hot wind blasts and limited availability of drinking water, had sapped their vitality. The news of the reinforcement of the base's defences had badly dented their morale.

The cave was a dry offshoot of a water-logged tunnel that in days gone by had served as a hiding place for aboriginal rebels and bushrangers fleeing from mounted police patrols. As Kate had surmised it was a well-guarded secret of the tribe on whose land it was located. Abdul welcomed its security and coolness but he was more accustomed to open forest terrain and being cooped up in a shadowy, torch-lit underground den was discomforting. He was further unnerved by the primitive paintings on the walls. Mike had told him they were so old that nobody knew anything for sure about the people and culture that had produced them.

He was putting a brave face on the news that his mission could not be completed because of the Australians' reinforcement of his target. But in a dark recess at the rear of the cave he felt free to let his true feelings of despair and shame flow over him which deepened his depression. He realised that this task was always likely to be a suicide mission as it was unlikely they would all escape and now, even worse, they might perish having failed to destroy their target. At times like this his only possible consolation was to turn to his God and laying his mat on the ground he took solace in the calming power of prayer. It granted him some relief from his troubled thoughts but he could not help feel the threat of a hidden spiritual presence in these caves that was even older than the birth of Islam. As he returned to join his men he was greeted by Mike.

"Good news Abdul I have just received a message that suggests your mission is not dead and that there is another way you can cripple the base without attacking it."

Abdul would not allow himself the indulgence of even faint hope until he had heard what Mike had to say and assessed its possibilities. Mike told him about the vulnerability of the base to losing its water supply and that as the aquifer pumping station was some way from the base and unguarded it would be easy to sabotage , giving them time to make their getaway. It seemed too good to be true but Abdul questioned Mike closely about the details of this option and also queried the provenance of the information.

"It came directly from your countryman who is in contact with Australian Military Intelligence. He has proved reliable up to now and using other sources, my cousin has checked that the aquifer is the only source of water supply and that it is vulnerable."

Abdul thanked him and gathered his non-coms around him to consider this news and decide whether and what to do about it. Kopassus forces, like their British and Australian SAS counterparts, were recruited as much for their intelligence and ingenuity as for their endurance and fighting qualities. He and his senior men had trained with the Australians and knew how devious and treacherous they could be when planning traps for their enemy. They agreed that the information was right but Abdul could not afford to risk all his people falling into a Norforce ambush.

It was agreed that they had to act on this intelligence, as they had no other option. But rather than commit all of his forces he formed a squad of four of his best men which he would lead to check out the source of the water supply and what it would take to knock it out.

"Check your weapons. Get some sleep as we will leave tonight. Ensure nothing in your kit will make a noise or reflect light and that you are camouflaged from head to foot. Sharpen your knives because any sentries we might encounter must be killed swiftly and silently before they can raise the alarm."

Hunters net their prey

Mike left the cave at dusk to send runners to Broome with news of Abdul's cautious plan. He was an excellent bushman and moved through the silent, moonless bush like a ghost that leaves not even a shadow. But good as he was Kate's watchers had lived all their lives in this country and as hunters they were alert to the passing of the stealthiest of prey. They chose not to take him at once but in accordance with Kate's orders they followed to see where he would go and who he would contact.

After an hour of cautious tracking they came upon the meeting of Mike with two men from their rival tribe. They were able to hear the gist of the conversation and when the meeting broke up they allowed the runners to depart safely so that the spies in Broome would believe that all was going to plan. But Mike was not so fortunate and as he followed a faint track out of the clearing he tripped over a cord stretched between two trees and was jerked into the air and hung upside-down from a tree branch, snared in a fibre net. For several minutes nothing else happened but just as he recovered from his surprise, he heard the murmurings of his ambushers below and shock gave way to fear. The men were from the tribe of the elder that the Kopassus had tortured and killed and he had no doubt that they would be eager to vent some of their vengeful anger on him.

The runners were far away and far beyond hearing when Mike's first shrieks of agony rent the silence of the night. Kate had stressed the need for information but had forbade them to kill him.

"That is the prerogative of the federal government." She said and "Despite the harm he and his type have done to us we must not act against the law." The Police at Halls Crossing had been alerted to expect a guest and were not surprised when a whimpering and badly scorched, Mike, was dumped on their door step. He was ferried from there under guard, to the base hospital and then back to Broome for further grilling by Military Intelligence, despite their expectation he had held little if any information back. His ultimate fate would be years in a maximum security prison followed by revocation of his citizenship and deportation to China.

Kate's thought mail message alerted Jane to the acceptance of the deception and vital intelligence about the make-up, intentions and hide-out of the Kopassus force that the tribesmen had extracted from the hapless Mike.

It was now her turn to take out Chang senior and his nest of traitors but this must wait until the message had reached the Man Fang cell and the runners were on their way back to the bush with messages of congratulation. Nonetheless she decided to reconnoitre the target to establish what force, if any, would be needed and to familiarise herself with the detailed lay out of the restaurant complex. She chose not to involve Ibrahim, so as not to compromise his double agent status when her force went in, and decided to start with some games of chance in the casino from which she could observe the restaurant entry.

There was nothing untoward in a lone Caucasian woman choosing to gamble so early in the evening and her boss had endorsed her plan without any concern for her safety. In fact she was on nodding acquaintance terms with some of the croupiers she had come across in the Food Bowl club and the chance passing of the restaurant's Maitre d' led to an invitation to be his guest for dinner when it opened in half an hour. This was working out better than she thought and even more so when she entered the restaurant and received an invitation to have a drink with the owner, Mr Chang in his V.I.P suite.

This was no cause for alarm as it was widely known that she and Ibrahim worked for the government Telecommunications Authority and Mr Chang's effusive welcome and attentive manner confirmed that, even if he suspected her secret role, he was sufficiently unconcerned to present no threat to her. They spent a pleasant hour chatting about her Asian experience and his obsession with his Jade collection. She had only accepted two cocktails and having politely declined a third she finished her drink and rose to go to dinner. As she walked towards the door that led to the dining room her eyes began to glaze over, her breathing quickened and before she could reach the door she fainted and fell to the richly carpeted floor.

Turning off the tap

Such was Abdul's training of his men that his reconnaissance patrol slipped undiscovered through the watcher cordon. GPS was unavailable but his hand compass guided them unerringly to their target without mishap. He was so suspicious of the information that they had received about the aquifer pump house, he had no intention of going directly to it without observing the target from a safe distance, in case there was an ambush awaiting them. His night vision glasses revealed no movement at the pump house nor could he detect any waiting Norforce troops. But having trained with Aussie SAS ambush experts, he had learned to respect their capacity for setting well-disguised traps.

He had brought along a friendly tribesman's hunting dog that had shown great affection for Abdul. Several hundred metres away from the site he released it and sent it loping towards the building. His intention was that it would sniff out any watchers but he had not anticipated the trigger rays that the dog passed through setting off flares that turned night into day over the aquifer outlet. A hail of small arms fire ripped through the trees decimating the foliage around the house. Abdul and his patrol fell back in quick order leaving the dog to race off into the bush and find its own way home. He was relieved to have his suspicions confirmed without losing a man and he prayed to Allah that they would be able to escape the area without being spotted.

Frank's men were puzzled not to find any casualties of their fire and even more puzzled by the lack of tracks until the dog's trail was spotted.

"Crafty buggers," spat the Sergeant Major. "We must have trained them right. They didn't just swallow the information we leaked to them. Best get after them before they get back to their cave and run into our main force."

Frank and the rest of his troop had stormed the cave where the Kopassus men had been holed up but all he found were the remains of their field rations and cold fire ashes. Turning to his lead tracker he issued fresh orders for the pursuit and contacted Kate in her camp.

"We missed them, Kate, they must have only half believed our story and they took the precaution of moving on in case we came for them. You need to scare up your best hunters and comb the area to ensure they do not find another hidden sanctuary. Now that we have taken out Chang they will know we are on to them so there is no reason to hold back on your rival tribe. Even though they are guilty of treason it would be more politically safe for your people to deal with them."

"Sorry to hear they got away Frank, don't worry about the traitors it will be a pleasure to settle some very old scores."

Before moving out, Frank tried to contact Jane but her thought mail failed to activate and he sped away after his men intending to try to call her again later.

Empty nest

When Frank's further attempts to catch Jane failed he began to be concerned and asked his commander to seek an explanation from Military Intelligence and an update on their move on the Man Fang spy nest. He was even more alarmed when news came back that her office had lost contact with her. It was known she had gone to the restaurant alone to check out the ground but that she had not contacted her office nor returned to her home. They were planning to raid the restaurant that very evening.

The raid was quick and forceful. All staff were arrested and guests were detained for questioning but there was no sign of Chang and his closest associates. The maitre'd confirmed that Jane had come for dinner and had drinks with the boss, but he had been too busy to notice when she had left. A thorough search revealed that all records had either been removed or burnt in an incinerator in the back yard. Amongst the ashes they found a scrap of bright coloured fabric that was identical to that which made up the dress Jane was wearing when she visited the restaurant.

Northern Strategic Command, Darwin

Growing alarm in Canberra and Coober Pedy about the time being taken to resolve the Kopassus threat to the base had necessitated an urgent meeting of the base defence task group with Northern Strategic Command officers to clarify and summarise the current situation. The commanding General rose to set the scene.

"Ladies and gentlemen, the Norforce strategy has not worked out as neatly as we had hoped. With the help of Chinese agents based in Broome and disaffected Kimberley Aboriginals, the Kopassus force has avoided decisive contact with the Norforce search and destroy team and is holed up somewhere in the vicinity of the Bungle Bungle base. The feeding of false decoy information to the enemy failed to lure them into a trap and a raid on the spies' headquarters in the Man Fang Restaurant, failed to capture any of them. They had decamped leaving no records nor indication as to where they had gone. Much worse is the likelihood that they have captured agent Jane Smith and taken her with them or, perish the thought, even murdered her."

"That is not a very encouraging summary for us to have to relay back to our military and political masters and I am sure I don't need to tell you that unless we can resolve this quickly and decisively there will be dire consequences for all of us involved."

"Your point is taken Admiral and at least there is the good news that we have surrounded the base with a heavily armed ready reaction force from Darwin, making it immune from the most direct attack."

"Thank you for small mercies General but what can we do to expedite our orders and totally remove this threat?"

"Now that we have decapitated the spy network and are in the process of dissuading the Aboriginal malcontents from aiding the enemy, all that remains is to hunt down and destroy the invading force. We have our finest Norforce men in the field under the command of Frank Bevan, whose capabilities are well known to you and they are backed up by the hunters and warriors of the tribe headed by Kate Carew. With all that expertise and local knowledge pitted against them it can't be long before we finish the job."

16

Search and Destroy

Jane goes bush

Jane was jolted awake by an abrupt break in the rolling gait of the camel on whose back she was tied. It took her some time to clear the cotton-wool feeling from her head and to remember that she had collapsed after drinking in the Man Fang. Obviously her drinks had been spiked and she cursed her unprofessional lack of caution in going to the restaurant unaccompanied and unarmed. Her behaviour had run counter to all that her instructors had drummed into her and that real death-cheating operational experience had hard wired into her tactical brain. As well as feeling guilty and ashamed, she began to feel the pain of her bonds and the uncomfortable pitch of the camel's tread. Shock set in when she realised she was not wearing the clothes she wore to the restaurant. Someone had undressed her and kitted her out in jeans, shirt and riding boots. For a moment she feared her person had been more brutally invaded but after careful consideration she could feel none of the expected discomfort in that quarter that sexual abuse would have caused. She flexed her hands and legs to test the strength of her bonds but instead of ropes they had used hard plastic ties which were unbreakable and which would resist all but a powerful cutter.

It seemed they had been travelling all night and as the sun came over the horizon she knew they were moving north and guessed they were heading for a contact on the coast from which they could be disembarked, with or without whoever was left of the Kopassus force. She assumed their failure to take the base would cause them to retreat and fight a running rear-guard action with Frank's team. But why had they encumbered themselves with her? Surely she had no value as a hostage and the government would not consider a ransom situation with so much at stake.

Her thoughts were disturbed by a rider who came alongside and seeing that she was awake, seized her camel's bridal and led them to a clearing on a river bank where she was helped to dismount and taken to sit with Chang on a rock by a cooking fire.

"Ah miss Smith," he exclaimed. "Good to have you back with us. Would you like some tea? I am afraid we only have black with a hint of eucalyptus leaf to spice up the river water."

She was parched and very glad to sip on the warm spicy tea. Feeling a little refreshed she demanded the release of her hands so that she could continue to drink unaided and when her request was granted, she turned to Chang and began to question his motives and actions.

"It is clear that you spiked my drink in your restaurant and now intend to exploit me as part of your escape plan. I would like to know why and where we are going."

Chang drew on his cigarette, tossed the remainder into the fire and turned to respond.

"We were never fooled by that communications role fairy tale. You were too assured and physically fit. We had heard from the Food bowl club staff about your skill in Asian languages-not really just a communications manager's attributes. Why have we captured rather than killed you? We appreciate you have no ransom value in the eyes of your government but we suspect Major Bevan might be persuaded to consider your safety should it come to a violent showdown."

"Now she knew what he intended, she saw no reason to continue the conversation and his treating her worse than he already had and so she clasped her mug of tea in both hands and turning her back on him, gazed into the fire desperately seeking inspiration about what she should do next.

Tribes at war

Kate was all for attacking the rival tribe with all the firepower her men had at their disposal. But after conferring with her elders and in particular the tribal medicine man, she was persuade that such an action would create a blood feud dispute that could fester for centuries and which could have incalculable consequences-not least the reaction from inner-city "progressives" and Canberra, if there were to be considerable loss of life.

At their urging she agreed to extract a dire retribution from their rivals for their support of those who had killed her father and the Wandjina restoration party. But they stressed that the process must be kept within the time honoured traditions of inter-tribal conflict. Although no member of the other tribe had actually been involved directly in the murders, they made a case for declaring a blood feud and determined to focus on its headman as the target for retribution. The vengeance party made ritual preparations, donning headbands, decorating their beards and painting on body stripes, before approaching the rivals' village.

They were expected and nobody was surprised when Kate's men refused the offer of reparations, rather than the surrender of their leader to execution. Having observed the niceties the party approached his hut to seize him but his tribe was aroused enough by this to gather round and form a defensive shield of hostility. In face of such overwhelming opposition, the avengers withdrew and returned to report the outcome of their failed raid. On the way back they came upon a little boy playing in the dust who told them that the chief had run away on the previous day. This news changed everything. To run away from traditional justice was a capital offence and now they had an even more solid pretext for opening up hostilities.

The aggrieved tribesmen saw their opportunity when a rival hunting party strayed across the boundary between their lands. At first, the fighting was with spears and the transgressors lost most of their men in the first two flights. At close quarters they slugged it out with war boomerangs. This short brutal affray led to more deaths on the rivals' side leaving a few disabled by concussion and superficial spear wounds. Amongst the dead were two sons of the chief and kate considered this sufficient pay- back to negotiate for an end to the conflict. The return of the few survivors and the bodies of the slain was a traumatic lesson for the village and reluctantly they opened talks to prevent a further massacre. They knew that in war time and because of their collusion with Australia's enemy, they could expect neither help nor sympathy from Canberra. Finally after lengthy wrangling they were forced to concede a slice of territory which secured the victors' rights to the land, up to the bank of the dividing river. In addition to wider hunting prospects it allowed them to share in the river's fishing bounty.

This was a very high price to pay even for treason but their capitulation had been ensured when Kate drew on the Wandjina's spirit by urging her medicine man to invoke powers of sorcery that would reinforce their physical triumph. On his visit to the place where his tribal elder had been murdered, he called to the spirit of the Wandjina, deep in the sacred pool, to bring down its wrath onto the offenders. Fear of sorcery still prevailed amongst indigenous people and this, even more than the threat of more deaths, sealed their surrender. Little did they know that this invocation of Wandjina power would have consequences much wider than the magical injunction against a tribe.

Indonesian embassy Canberra

"Ambassador the news from the Kimberley is not good and our Chinese friends will not be pleased. The Kimberley signalling station has been reinforced to a level that makes it impossible for the Kopassus to complete their mission. They are in hiding but this may soon be exposed, as the help they are receiving from a friendly tribe has been cut off by attacks from a rival tribe loyal to their government. Even worse, the Chinese spy base in the Kimberley has been raided and although the spy chief has escaped towards the coast the network of undercover agents is being rounded up for interrogation, as we speak. In other words the Australians know all our secrets and there seems to be no possibility of crippling the base"

"So, Chief, what can we do? What are our options?"

"We only have one option. We must get a message to the Kopassus commander to cut his losses and retreat in the best possible order to rendezvous with the escaping spies at the extraction point on the Kimberley coast."

"Thank you. I will confer with Djakarta to establish Chinese concurrence with this plan and to despatch a submarine to take everyone off when they have reached the coast."

Hide and seek

Frank was doubly troubled. He could not find the Kopassus hideout and he had heard that Jane had been taken and possibly murdered by the Chinese spies. There was nothing he could do to help Jane but hope she was still alive. But his prime consideration had to be the elimination of the Kopassus threat. Military Intelligence had advised him that Abdul Supomo was in command of the Indonesian troops and Frank remembered meeting him on joint training exercises during his SAS days. It helped to put a face to his counterpart and from what he could remember of him in action, Abdul was a thinking soldier and despite Kopassus's reputation for ruthless brutality he would do his damnedest to get as many of his men home as possible.

Kate had advised him of the outcome of the tribal war and that the Broome spies were on the run. This meant that Abdul was on his own and could expect no outside help to guide him to safety.

Putting himself in Abdul's shoes, what would he do? All he could come up with was to acquire horses or camels from the friendly tribe and travel by forced night stages towards a submarine rendezvous on the coast.

Power play

Abdul was of the same mind and he had conscripted from the defeated tribe sufficient horses for he and his men to ride and pack camels to carry their heaviest gear and water. Their base was a little known canyon just outside the Purnalulu Park which had a fresh water supply and was camouflaged by dense palms, shielding them from the prying lenses of overhead drones. The escape route would be long and arduous. He could only move by night and despite all his men's training and skills in camouflaged and silent movement it would be hard to evade Norforce scouts. There was bound to be bitter fighting. But he had done his duty to the best of his ability, he had made his peace with God, and was resigned to ending his days in this alien land. He was even more disconcerted in the last few days by increased awareness of a malevolent presence hovering around them and he had noticed that his men had become unusually addicted to prayer.

Late on the afternoon of their intended departure his pickets returned to camp accompanying the most extraordinary figure. He was dressed in the tattered and journey-stained garb of a traditional Afghan cameleer and led a string of three pack camels, laden with camp gear and strange equipment that appeared to be of an electronic nature. In response to Abdul's customary welcome greeting the stranger muttered a guttural G'day through tight lips which were dry and blistered by over exposure to the topical sun. It was obvious that he had travelled far across harsh country and that he was badly in need of shelter, food and water and a safe place to rest in.

Abdul was alarmed by his intrusion but was also sufficiently intrigued by his dress to hold off his interrogation until the man was in a better condition to answer for himself and stayed the hand of his sergeant who was primed to slit the man's throat. It was still well before dark and so there was plenty of time for the man to be refreshed enough to start talking and to determine his fate before their scheduled departure time.

In response to Abdul's opening questions about who he was and what he was doing wandering the Kimberly alone in time of war, the man cupped his hands possessively around his billy of sweet tea and began to tell the most remarkable tale.

"My name is George Atkins and you probably have never heard of me but you would have done if you had been following the Australian nuclear power political debates back in the '20s when the government opted for the building of remote nuclear power plants around the Australian coast."

His English was good but his accent was indeterminate, neither broad Australian nor British, although it might have been based on one of those peculiar dialects that Abdul had heard were still alive in parts of the UK. This initial response was sufficiently intriguing for him to give the man free rein and he nodded to encourage the man to continue his story.

"Whilst the debate was at its height I was a little known exploration geologist but when I discovered a massive uranium deposit in the Kimberley region, my nomadic wandering in search of mineral wealth in the wild outback regions became the subject of magazine articles and even a TV series. I achieved fame overnight and on the strength of the decision to switch to clean, green, nuclear power I was foolish enough to try to become a real swashbuckling romantic hero by founding a get rich quick exploration company and exploiting my TV exposure for all it was worth."

"You look a real wild romantic now but certainly not a rich one." Interjected Abdul.

"You are so right. I made all the usual mistakes. Floated at the wrong time, bet everything I had on the Uranium price, overindulged in wine and women, especially women. More discoveries and oversupply led to a market crash which wiped me out. Like the real life coward I am, I fled the news hounds and my creditors by escaping to the bush and became so enamoured of the free life, I have been a wanderer out here ever since and have landed-up as you see me now. But before I answer any more of your questions, which you are entitled to ask having rescued me from a bad situation, who are you guys and what are you doing out here?"

Abdul had anticipated just such a question and had prepared a convincing story. Before they left their submarine all his men had removed identifying insignia from their uniforms and the subsequent days living rough in the bush had added grime to make them look no different from any soldiers exercising in the bush.

"We are a Nato contingent on a real live fire exercise with your Australian Norforce Regiment. We are acting as the enemy and they are hunting us. As you can see we are packing up to move on tonight to keep one jump ahead of them. We are learning so much from this exercise in such hard, trackless country and what a climate!"

The man readily accepted this answer and Abdul continued his questioning trying to test the man's story and trip him up by repeating similar queries in different ways. But his every response was consistent and convincing. Finally he mused on the universal success of nuclear power.

"Sure there was much talk about and experimenting with environmentally pure alternative energy sources but governments almost went broke trying to keep up the subsidy payments and placate angry voters whose power bills went up and up without pause. I guess you know that just about every activity of any size which demands considerable quantities of electrical power is nuclear dependent and one day soon houses will have their own mini units just like their external air conditioning equipment."

Abdul believed he was the innocent party he claimed to be but with the lives of his men at risk he could not take any chances and left the decision whether to let him go on his way or more likely ensure his silence by killing him, until they had finished dinner and were ready to go. They left the stranger to his personal toilet some distance away in the bush and went to dinner by the smokeless fire over which Kangaroo haunches had been roasted to perfection.

After completing his ablutions and evening prayers Abdul sat quietly reflecting on the task ahead when a startling realisation came to him. The wanderer had said that almost every major activity requiring considerable electrical power was nuclear dependent-but what about the Communications base. Where did its power come from? Leaping up he dashed to where the man was sitting drying his hair and sitting down across from him asked him about the base's power source.

"Why of course, such a power hungry facility as that had to be nuclear powered but for safety reasons the power generator was located about a kilometre away and was shielded from the base by several canyons and rocky ridges. The base certainly couldn't function without it."

Abdul was so excited by this news he failed to acknowledge his informant and sprinted back to call a meeting of his Sergeants which soon began to consider a resumption of their mission with the nuclear unit as their target. When they had agreed on a plan of action Abdul asked for the prospector to be brought to him to provide detailed directions to the nuclear facility. But when his man returned he was without the prospector and reported there was no sign of the man nor his camels. Abdul ordered an instant search of the area round the camp and especially the routes he might have followed. But the hard ground held no clues, especially as the camels were so soft footed and there was no sign of his passing on the several routes he might have taken.

Abdul cursed his lack of professionalism in not putting the

visitor under guard and now that darkness had fallen there was no chance of their catching up with such a skilled bushman and it would necessitate scattering his men far and wide and risking instant detection by Norforce or Aboriginal scouts. Nevertheless he believed the story and determined to send two of his best trackers in the general direction the man had indicated and check the plant was really there and how well it was guarded.

When his men returned and confirmed its existence and location he was elated but somewhat more sceptically surprised to hear its only protection was two sentries with light armaments who were idling in a nearby hut. Abdul reconvened his planning meeting and scheduled their attack for the following night. At first light a patrol brought him a piece of what proved to be a strip of cloth torn from the prospector's turban by a thorn on an overhead tree branch. Its location confirmed he had moved away from their position in a direction that would avoid his coming across the Norforce searchers and he would certainly not want to fall in with more grim looking armed men. This made him easier about delaying his attack by a day as he was sure he would only get one chance and it had to be perfectly planned and executed.

17

Base Attack

A tell-tale sign

Chang and his party continued on to their coastal rendezvous point. Jane's legs had been freed but her hands were still cuffed and there was little chance of her getting away from them in the pitch dark bush which was totally alien to her.

She had listened carefully to their conversations and established that the order to pull out had been given and that the plan was to extract them from the coast in a Chinese submarine. Where exactly she was not sure. Whilst she appreciated that her kidnapping would not attract a government ransom she was sure they would send searchers after them to capture Chang and any Kopassus who might have evaded Frank's Norforce hunters. She felt powerless to escape or slow them down but then she could leave clues for the pursuit. On the journey she had picked up a sharp flint stone and at each stopping point she scratched the letters SOSJ. Into the trunk of nearby trees.

Ibrahim's Jihad

Ibrahim had been mortified by the news of Jane's abduction and the more he thought about where she might be and what they could do to her, he felt enormous guilt about his role in causing her to be involved in this plot. The Spy ring had disappeared without contacting him and now that he was completely out of the information loop his contact at the Indonesian embassy disowned him and swore him to silence on pain of his relatives deaths.

Jane's boss was responsive to his enquiries but could or would not impart too much information about moves to rescue her and was entirely unsympathetic to his angst and willingness to help in any way he could.

In desperation he turned to his last resort, his religion and his all merciful God. He prayed intensely for guidance and even confided to an extent in a local Imam in Broome. After days of fasting and prayer it came to him that he should invoke a Jihad or sacred mission to help recover Jane alive and in doing so achieve some redemption for the evil that he had done.

But what could he do? He was neither a bushman nor a fighter and now that the spies had gone there was no way he could find out what they intended. He decided to drown his sorrows by joining his new friends at the Food Bowl Club but even there enquiries about why Jane was not with him caused him further pain and shame.

Then he spotted a young woman whom he had met at the Indonesian consulate. Crossing to where she was sitting he asked her to dance. She was a rather a plain and retiring young woman and she was surprised and delighted to be partnered onto the floor by this handsome and well known Lothario. She danced well and they spent a good deal of the evening on the dance floor. He had decided to go carefully and at the end of the evening he thanked her and suggested that they might dine together one evening soon. Her look suggested she might have welcomed an extension of that evening's flattery and flirting and she readily agreed and mentioned the evenings on which she was free. Ibrahim proposed a date and said he would make a booking and let her know the time and place. He had not mentioned her work whilst dancing but he had ascertained that she worked in the signals section and handled confidential communications between Broome, Melbourne and Djakarta.

Their dinner date went well and whatever reserve there might have been between them was melted by Ibrahim's charm. He was not to have the sort of success he was accustomed to with western women and although she was bowled over by him the inhibitions implanted by her very conservative parents kept her from going to his bed. But she certainly dropped her veil in respect of work intelligence and confirmed that she had transmitted and translated messages to the effect that the spies were planning a departure by sea and that although the Kopassus mission had seemed to fail and the troops had been recalled, there was a secret coded message she couldn't fully access, to the effect that a final opportunity might have opened up to disable the base.

Ibrahim was elated and though he regretted not being able to sample her delights he kissed her goodnight, confirmed another date and then sped round to Military Intelligence to impart his news. He was well received because he was a step ahead of what they had heard from Frank, who was still searching for the departing enemy.

Confirmation on a camel

The prospector had not departed in the direction that his torn turban fragment had suggested and when one of Frank's scouts found him brewing a billy of tea over the ashes of his campfire he was more than ready to go along with him to yet again explain his strange appearance and presence in that wilderness.

Franks' first shock occurred when he approached the stranger and holding out his hand, said, "G'day mate, my name's Frank Bevan I am the leader of this Norforce patrol."

The stranger ignored his hand, stretched to his full height and with a slight bow and clicking of his heels responded,

"Glad to meet you Major. My name is Boris Maximilian Udanov lately a Major in a Russian 'Spetsnaz', special-forces, regiment and now a secret agent in the Russian Security Service, which you will know as the FSB."

"What the hell are you doing here? A bit off your patch isn't it?"

"I am here at the express invitation of the CIA and with the support of your ASIO. I have been here for some months acting as a shadow agent supporting your defence of the base by monitoring the activities of Chinese field agents such as Mike Chang and making their lives difficult by sowing distrust and enmity amongst the local tribes."

"For Christ's sake, you have been out there all the time backing us up and we were not told?"

"Nor was your Military Intelligence. My mission was requested by the Americans because they so value your remaining signals base that whilst they have every confidence in your ability on your own patch they thought it would be good to give you some insurance as the Chinese were pitting so many resources against you. Also, after what the Chinese have done to my country, I am delighted to be here and at your service. I guess your ASIO doesn't always confide in its agencies."

"But why you, a Russian, in Australia? It's a bit like sending me to operate in Siberia."

"Not so strange really my friend when you know my background. My military service was in the Caucasus where you will know we have been hard pressed to keep the lid on the Islamic extremists in the breakaway republics spilling over into our territories. It has been so for more than two centuries when we played the great game against the British on India's Himalayan frontier. I became so adept at moving amongst Islamic tribes, speaking their languages and riding a camel, that I was seconded to the FSB as a field agent. You will have noticed my dark and swarthy appearance-I am Part Georgian and part Tatar and this added to my disguise. So, navigating your bush and living off the land was not such a great hardship for me and I even fooled the Kopassus."

"You have met them?"

"Oh yes. Just as they were about to pull out and head for the coast for extraction. But I was able to stop that and gave them a new hope of crippling the base which has prevented them leaving and given you a further chance to finish them off when they attack."

"You did what! I thought you were supposed to be on our side. What did you tell them that changed their minds?"

When Boris had explained how he had sown the seed about the vulnerability of the power plant, Frank was aghast.

"What made you do that and undermine our successful defence of the base?"

"Steady friend-all is not what it at first seems in the espionage game and we Russians are pretty experienced. You will recall Winston Churchill's famous verdict on Russia that it 'is a riddle wrapped in a mystery inside an enigma.' My leaking of this information was deliberate and sanctioned at the highest levels of your intelligence command. The power plant is a dispensable decoy which needs to be destroyed to lull the Chinese into the false belief that the base is truly crippled and that all the western allies detection and control systems are blind."

"But isn't that a massive price to pay to deceive the Chinese and how does this help our side?"

"No. The power plant is redundant. Technological advances have allowed the base to be powered by a smaller nuclear source that could be based safely and therefore more securely, within the base complex deep under the mountain. So, blowing up the power plant will not cripple the base but when Kopassus do it, the base will fake going off line and they and the Chinese will be convinced they have trumped your ace card."

"But I still don't understand. How can this help us win the war?"

"That I do not know. Such considerations are way above my pay grade and yours too no doubt."

"What a tangled web. But how do we know they will buy this deception of yours?"

"They already have. One of the signals staff at the Indonesian Consulate in Broome has confirmed to your double agent, Ibrahim, that there is another possible way of destroying the base. A Kopassus scouting party has reconnoitred the site of the plant and found it lightly guarded by a few soldiers dressed in Norforce uniforms."

"You certainly seem to have covered all the bases but where does that leave me and my men?"

"Expect fresh orders by your ingenious thought mail at any minute."

When the orders came they were the strangest he had ever received and ran counter to all his training and the regiment's tradition of aggressive reconnaissance and ruthless attack.

"So what are your orders Major?" Boris enquired.

"We are to put up a semblance of defence as though we are caught completely by surprise and then we must allow them to escape unmolested but closely monitored as they retreat to their escape point. I must say this goes against all our training and the boys will not be best pleased. I had better brief them right away."

Do no harm

Frank was right, the men were not pleased and it took some persuading as well as a call on discipline to prevent their setting out to massacre the whole Kopassus force in vengeance for the murder of their fellow tribe's leader. Then he spelled out the ground rules he had been ordered to follow.

"We must allow them to destroy the power house and escape with minimal casualties, believing that they have closed down the base. Now let's plan how best to do this."

Power house attack

Abdul was determined not to be caught out twice and although he believed what he had been told about the power house and had it verified by his own men he planned to proceed cautiously and avoid another Norforce trap. His demolition expert had determined how much explosive would be needed to destroy the placeand where the charges should be set. Each of his men had carried some of the explosive materials they would be likely to need on the mission and no doubt they would be glad of reducing some of their load for the journey back. All the materials had been combined to make up four bombs which would be detonated by remote control at the farthest distance from the plant that their trigger device would work. The bombs were to be placed on strategic parts of the power house by two men while the rest took up supporting fire positions in case Norforce should but in.

Abdul sweated with apprehension and fear as his men approached their target. Not only his honour but perhaps the whole outcome of the war depended on the success of this attack. A scout had preceded them and reported back that the sentries were not there and this had heightened Abdul's concern that he might be the victim of another ambush but all went according to plan. The demolition men returned and reported the bombs were in place, allowing a relieved Abdul to order a careful tactical withdrawal to the detonation point.

To ensure they made a flying start ahead of the inevitable Norforce pursuit following on the explosion, the majority of his men rode away on horseback, towing the pack camels, whilst he and the demolition man stayed back to detonate the bombs. Half an hour after they had moved off, there was no sign of any Norforce activity and Abdul signalled for the bombs to be exploded. Much work had gone into reducing the noise of their munitions, without reducing their destructive force and the muffled "crump" of each of the four explosions confirmed that they had done their job and it was time to ride hell for leather out of there and catch up with his team.

After twelve hours of nonstop travel through the dried out savannah landscape he called a halt where they could hide, sheltered by a series of rocky outcrops and sent a message with one of the remaining loyal Aboriginal runners to an agent hidden in Halls Creek. It told his superiors that the mission had been a complete success and that the base was crippled by loss of power. Although the Chinese technicians could still not pinpoint the base's location, they were able to ascertain that no signals were coming from that part of Australia and by hacking into US military signals they confirmed the consternation of the Americans at losing their last defence signals capability.

Cool pursuit

Frank followed his orders to the letter. He knew where the fleeing Kopassus men were at all times and when they were able to slip away from his men in the dead of moonless nights, Kate's hunters kept tabs on them. The base had carried out a mock shut-down as though the power had really been cut off but they were preparing for whatever their masters would demand of them when they were ordered to switch on again.

Frank had to take sufficient action to convince the Kopassus that they were being pursued but he was ordered that under no account was he to prevent their journey to the sea nor must he kill Abdul who when captured would be tried for the murder of the Aboriginal elder and paraded before the world's media as a war criminal. Frank complied but found proceeding in a half-hearted manner was even harder than going in hard. His men ensured the Indons knew they were being followed and he allowed his snipers to take out one of them and fell a horse and a camel. He was assured that when they got to their rendezvous with their extraction team, all the Kopassus raiders and the Chinese spies would be rounded up and hopefully the navy would bag a Chinese nuclear sub.

Abdul could not understand the ineffectiveness of the Norforce pursuit but he was nonetheless grateful and happy to bask in the reflected glory of his achievement. His prayers were full of thanks rather than supplication and he felt a growing belief that they might actually get back alive. All that lay between them and salvation was Australia's best defence against invaders, the land itself and crossing the tinder dry Kimberley was a daunting challenge in itself. Water was becoming increasingly hard to find and their field rations were perilously low. The horses were suffering as a result of the relentless pace but the camels trudged on seemingly impervious to the heat and their loads. He vowed not to drop his guard. One slip and no matter how badly Norforce seemed to be performing they would be despatched without mercy because of what they had done to the Aboriginal idol painters. He felt guilt for this action and although he dismissed it as a trick of a tired mind, he still felt the continuing presence of a malevolent force emanating from the surrounding rocks and trees. Clouds were appearing for the first time and he wondered why when the monsoon rains were not due for months.

18

Kimberley Kill

Pointing the way

As they were far from any habitation and confident that Jane could not get far if she escaped into the bush, Chang had freed her of her bonds and she was able to walk about the camp under the watchful gaze of the Chinese guards. Whilst she had received survival training she was not confident of making her way through this waterless wilderness and she had not yet found out where they were headed.

On the next day, instead of proceeding parallel to the river they verged sharply right on a faint track that would lead them into the river gorge, farther back from the sea than she had anticipated. There were no suitable trees to mark here but she had to ensure the followers did not just ride past. Feigning the need for a toilet stop she walked into the bushes and as she came out and the men who kept watch on her turned their backs to mount their horses, she pinned her bra under a heavy stone on a roadside termite mound. It would be hard to miss as it was bright pink. The Norforce trooper who was to find this marker would dine out on the story for years to come in the regimental mess and raise guffaws when he swore he didn't know that bras grew in the wild.

That night, Jane crept up on the campfire of a group of marines who were discussing the plan to make use of the huge tidal variations. She heard that they already had hover boats hidden down by the river ready to leave on the outgoing tidal surge as soon as the kopassus party caught up. On the following day, just before dinner, Abdul and his weary party came in. The men were gaunt and their uniforms were in tatters. After a refreshing splash in the river they kept the camp cooks busy filling them up with real food-a blessed relief after field rations.

Abdul saw them settled and didn't bother to bathe or eat. After giving thanks for their deliverance in his prayers he lay on his swag and fell into a deep sleep.

Jane had to act, as they were planning to leave on the next tide. She had not tried to run off and deliberately displaying predictable patterns of behaviour she had succeeded in lulling her guards into a false sense of security. At night she would take a shovel full of coals and start a small fire in a quiet corner of the camp on which she would boil her billy for tea. When she had done this she came back to the cooking area where the hard pressed cooks had generated more fat from the meat cooking than usual and they had placed buckets full of the waste fat under some trees in a dark spot. Jane sidled by when they were intent on their grillers and carried off a full bucket which she took into the surrounding bush and liberally coated as many trees as possible with the combustible fat and threw the residue onto the dry grasses.

Grabbing a warm top to keep out the night chill she shovelled up some glowing coals from her fire and slipping stealthily into the trees she threw the coals onto the fat soaked timber. She began to run as fast as the darkness and rough terrain would allow but she had only put fifty metres or so between herself and the camp when the bush exploded with light from a curtain of flame that spread rapidly, fanned by a brisk evening breeze

The marines and Kopassus soldiers feared they were under attack and began firing indiscriminately into the blazing surrounding bush. Abdul woke in alarm and he was soon joined by Chang in attempting to re-impose order.

Frank's force was not far away and the fire was like a beacon to him. He did not wonder what had caused it but he urged his men on to see what advantage it might offer him in launching his attack. At least it had confirmed the message of the bra that they were planning to be lifted off up river rather than from the more obvious coastal inlets. No wonder the Navy was having problems where to concentrate their patrols.

The Wandjina wakes

Kate had complete faith in Frank and Norforce to avenge her father by destroying the Kopassus invaders but she needed a role in this act of vengeance for her tribe and to prevent the hot-headed young men risking their lives needlessly. The answer had to be sorcery.

She summoned the council of tribal elders and after deep discussion the medicine man was despatched to the Wandjina wall and sacred pool. What he did there, she would never know. But by the look on his face when he returned he was very pleased with his effort to enlist the powers of the Wandjina.

All-out assault

Frank drew his men around him. He could see the blood lust in their eyes and grim faces. He knew that he had held them under tight control for long enough and that they would be satisfied with nothing less than the chance to kill Kopassus murderers and avenge the killing of Kate's father and their desecration of the Wandjina site.

"Now is your chance to destroy the Kopassus force but I must caution you that our rules of engagement must be honoured-there will be no killing of any who surrender or are wounded. We are professionals, not savage mercenaries. Any man who breaches this code will face a court martial and you know what that means in time of war. But you are free to kill, in self-defence, any who resist. I am under strict orders from the Prime Minister to take their Commander alive, so that he can stand trial as a war criminal.

So, even if he fights back, and he sure will, disable him but do not kill him. Understood?"

He noted their unanimous nods of assent and when he issued orders for the attack, the silence of the night was broken by the click of weapons being primed and the clack of bayonets being fixed into place. Frank needed to release his own pent up frustration but although he wanted to destroy the Kopassus unit as a fighting force he was determined not to squander the lives of his magnificent men.

His opening move was to launch a flight of back-pack drones. Some to hover above the camp and reveal through their night vision cameras the disposition of the forces in the rock ledge camp. Abdul and Chang could be seen making desperate efforts to bring their panicking men under control and frank noted the addition of marines to the defending force.

"Ok guys let's give them something to really panic bout."

In instant response to his command a second flight of drones fired their deadly missiles down into the camp killing many marines before they could take cover and blowing Chang to pieces. They followed up with a withering fire from all the automatic weapons in the Norforce armoury which left few defenders able or willing to put up a fight. The intensity of the fire-fight stripped branches from the surrounding trees and shredded their trunks. It looked as though a cyclone had torn through the gorge. As planned, Abdul and his Sergeant body-guard were allowed to retreat into the shelter of a rock overhang screened by a cluster of large boulders.

Frank understood that a prolonged siege could only end in Abdul's death or that he might even commit suicide rather than face the dishonour of capture. He signalled for covering fire and jinked and swerved his way across the intervening ground and took shelter against one of the boulders screening the enemy position. Before Abdul had time to react he hurled a succession of stun and flash grenades over into the space behind the boulders, under the overhang and raced in to finish the job.

The grenades had done their job, temporarily blinding and deafening Abdul and his Sergeant. Both were curled up on the ground with sore eyes tight shut and nursing their ravaged ears. He tethered Abdul hand and foot with nylon cords and kneeling by the prone Commander paused to catch his breath and still his pounding heart whilst his men captured the NCO.

Lost and found in the bush

Jane had blundered through the pitch dark bush crashing into trees and tripping over logs. She had no idea where she was nor where she was going. She just wanted to get as far as possible away from any pursuit. There was no sound of followers and needing to get her second wind she stopped crashing blindly through the darkness and slumped down onto a log. Her breathing and heart beat had just about returned to normal when a hand was clamped over her mouth and she was lifted off the ground in the strong arms of Aboriginal warriors. She was petrified and desperately sought a means of fighting back when their leader whispered into her ear.

"Don't be afraid. We are friends sent by Kate Carew to look out for you. I am going to remove my hand so please nod your understanding and do not make a sound because our enemy is close by.

"Thank Heaven", Jane whispered, "I was completely lost and feared I might die out here and never be found."

"You are safe with us but, listen!"

The noise of rocket explosions and gunfire at the camp carried to them and turning in that direction she urged her rescuers to lead her to where the battle was raging.

End game

Frank had dropped to his knees to check on Abdul's breathing. Half turning in response to a loud crunching of gravel behind him

Frank saw the Sergeant charging towards him intent on impaling Frank on his lunging bayonet. Locked in a crouch there was nothing he could do to escape this awful end and closing his eyes and gritting his teeth he anticipated the deadly thrust.

Instead he heard a loud gurgling noise and the thud of something heavy hitting the ground. Opening his eyes he was amazed to see the Sergeant lying flat on his back, clutching in vain at the handle of a vicious fighting knife that was embedded in his throat, as his life ebbed away.

"Thank God" gasped Dan before he succumbed to a terrible shivering fit.

"Don't thank God. Just be grateful I topped my training group in knife throwing."

"Jane, he yelled. You are alive and you saved my life!" Then before hysteria overcame him Jane ran to him, embraced him tenderly and assured him all was well.

"For a moment there I thought I had lost you so soon after finding you and as I want you in my life I just did for him in the nick of time."

"What a strange and wonderful woman you are to kill a man so ruthlessly to save the one you want. What can I say but that I am all yours." He could say no more as shock overcame him and he fell into a protective slumber.

19

Gods of war

Storm force

The enemy body count was grim. All the marines and all but Abdul and one of his Kopassus troopers had perished. Two Norforce men had suffered minor wounds and one boat carrying Chinese spies was escaping with the outgoing tide. Frank was so relieved that Jane was alright, proud of his men's professionalism and happy that he had taken Abdul alive.

He was standing talking with his Sergeant discussing the transfer of the captives to Broome when a loud commotion broke out in the direction of the river. A breathless soldier ran up to him and gasped out.

"Sir, Abdul had a concealed knife we failed to find. He has cut himself free and is descending the gorge wall towards the boats and he is holding Miss Smith hostage with his knife at her throat."

Frank's heart sank. He had just become accustomed to having found her safe and sound and now he might lose her in this cruel way. Grabbing his weapon and followed by a platoon of his fighters Frank sprinted to the edge of the gorge where his worst fears were confirmed.

Abdul was standing on a ledge just a few metres below the gorge rim. He had a secure grip on Jane and was holding a large hunting knife across her throat. He was screaming insanely about his successful mission and the will of God. Frank could see no easy way of rescuing Jane without killing Abdul and even though his expert snipers could shoot at him, in the low light they risked hitting Jane or not wounding Abdul sufficiently to prevent his slitting her throat.

He was about to order a head shot when the clear night sky was lit up by the most dramatic electric light show. Lightening shattered the sky's placid surface like a brick hitting a pane of glass and strikes set fire to the tinder dry bush all around them. A fierce cyclonic wind howled up the river gorge and torrential rain of Monsoonal force poured down from a cloudless sky. Within minutes every dry gully, spring and tributary of the Isdell spewed their run-off from the plateau into the river sending a torrential wall of water surging down-stream, picking up boulders, sucking trees into the flood, sweeping away the escaping hover boat and drowning all aboard.

Frank had taken shelter with his men behind the rocks and under the overhang from which Abdul had tried to repel their attack and when the mighty monsoonal downpour stopped as abruptly as it had started, he ran back to the edge of the river gorge and saw with relief that Abdul and Jane were above the flood level and had escaped a watery grave. They were clinging together as though stuck with glue and both were sodden and born down by their exposure to the storm. Frank was about to run down the slope and rescue Jane but Abdul was not yet done and finding sufficient reserves of strength to rise to his feet, he resumed his insane ranting, whilst still threatening Jane with his knife.

He heard the scuff of Frank's boots as he stepped onto the slope and took his eyes off Jane for the split second she needed to fall to the ground, as if in a faint, pivot on her arse and deliver a vicious kick to Abdul's right leg just below the knee cap. The crack of breaking bone could be heard by all up on the edge but although he staggered and howled with pain he was still strong enough to stay on his feet and point his knife down at Jane. Frank raised his weapon and was about to get off a shot at Abdul when, with the chilling scream of a banshee, a turbaned figure garbed all in white, emerged from the long grass, ran at Abdul and clasping him close in a vice-like embrace cried out,

"Allahu Akbar!" and leaped off the ledge taking Abdul with him in an unbreakable embrace of death. Despite the darkness the white figure could be seen spinning and tumbling through the air as the pair plunged towards the roaring river maelstrom and disappeared beneath its waves. Ibrahim had achieved his Jihad and made good his desire for redemption.

"Poor Ibrahim. May he rest in peace." Jane whispered, before she passed out in Frank's arms and he and two of his men carried her back up to the safety of the edge of the gorge.

Bringer of life giving rain

Kate had heard of the unseasonable storm and its outcome with quiet satisfaction. She was back at her work in the Bungle Bungle base, which was busily preparing for some special, top-secret action. Before she had left her village she had sent a party of elders with the medicine man to revisit the Wandjina and finish the restoration work interrupted by her father's murder. Theirs was the time honoured duty of making supplications to the spirits in the pool that the life-bringing Monsoon rains would come again, on time and in due season.

20

War no more

Bungle Bungle base

Deep under the mountain range the communications base was a hive of activity. It was about to go on-line again. Large video screens showed the disposition of Chinese and North Korean naval, air and missile units. The Commander stood beside the main control console from which he sent messages to Australian and US military commands detailing movements of enemy forces. His phone rang and all eyes in the control room turned to him as he concurred with his caller.

"Yes General, certainly. We will take immediate action in accordance with your orders which I understand have the blessing of the war Cabinet"

Putting down the phone and looking directly at Jane he gave the order.

"Let's light up people and get back on-line. This is our big chance to make a final difference in this war."

Australian War Cabinet Room, Coober Pedy

After a cabinet meeting that had gone throughout the night, interrupted by frequent exchanges with the President of the United States and the Prime Ministers of the UK, Canada, India and Japan, the Australian Prime Minister took his seat at a table backed by the national flag. Looking directly into the cameras, power and TV services having been restored a few hours earlier, he spoke to the nation in a tired, but confident and reassuring voice.

"My fellow Australians. At Eight pm last night the combined military forces of the Asian Axis powers were about to launch a mass attack on our military installations and major cities. Thanks to the work of our combined intelligence services they did not take us by surprise and an overwhelming pre-emptive counter strike from all our services, including US space-based missiles, totally destroyed the enemy's capacity to continue to wage war, without inflicting undue damage on their population centres.

As a consequence the Chinese and North Korean governments have surrendered unconditionally. A general armistice has been proclaimed and hostilities have ceased. The crippling Middle-Eastern war has been fought to a devastating standstill and a new re-alignment of trans-national governments under the auspices of the UN will be established and energy exports will be resumed as soon as war damage has been repaired. China will withdraw all military forces from Siberia immediately and an international conference will convene to negotiate reparations.

Nearer to home our neighbour Indonesia, with which we have enjoyed prolonged cordial relations, is to sign a peace and prosperity pact with us which will greatly favour our agricultural and energy export industries.

Finally I must pay tribute to all who fought and died to preserve our freedoms and I specially commend our Kimberley Defence Communications base which remained active throughout the war and the Norforce regiment which secured it against the possibility of enemy attack.

Ladies and gentlemen. The war is over!"

Midnight in Moscow

Grigor Ribokov and his colleagues had received an unexpected summons back to duty by Military Intelligence and he was not pleased to have had to abandon his latest girlfriend to the tender mercies of his rivals at his favourite night club.

"Here we go again. Another night ruined and for what?"

But as he spoke all the computer monitors began to spark back into life and with wonder and increasing excitement they ran to their familiar screens to see the welcome return of the pictures and data on which their analytical work depended.

"On second thoughts, you fellows. I'd rather be here to see this, especially the Chinese retreating from Siberia with their tails between their legs, than waste my life in that flea-bitten bar that pretends to be a night-club. Long live Russia. Long may we be free!"

21

Kimberley cattle station

A place to stay

Frank still liked to ride out on his horse to watch the cattle muster, even though the bulk of the herding was done on hover bikes and helo-jets. Dismounting from the saddle on the top of a high bluff he surveyed with great satisfaction and pride the vast sweep of his property, greened and well watered by the recent wet season.

Food exports were in high demand to feed starving people in the war ravaged Middle East and China, burdened with massive war reparation payments to Russia. His cattle business was growing fast and proving to be very profitable. Riding back into the homestead yard he walked his horse to the stables and asked the farrier to check a couple of loosening shoes. As he returned to the house he spotted a small cloud of dust along the road leading to the main gate, which appeared to be kicked up by two supply camels and he wondered at such a strange and old fashioned way of bringing the mail and supplies.

He thought no more of it until he had taken off his boots and entered the house intent on a bath and a change into fresh clothes, when he heard a vaguely familiar voice bellowing.

'Where is the boss of this outfit? Frank Bevan, what sort of bush hospitality is this not to greet an old friend who has suffered such hardships to come and visit you? You might at least slake my thirst with a glass or two of your finest malt whisky."

Frank flung wide the front door and as he stepped onto the veranda he was clamped in a Russian bear hug and replied in kind.

"Boris you silly bastard. What are you doing here and what made you come unannounced? Anyway, welcome and come in for more than one scotch."

"Thank you Frank. I like Australia so much I have decided to – how do you say it? – Migrate? No more Siberian snows for me. The Australian Government has shown its gratitude for the small war service I did and has seen fit to grant me immediate citizenship. But don't worry I am not looking for a job with you. I have come to fulfil a sacred duty by escorting a very special guest to your station."

Boris stood aside and gestured for Frank to step forward. The sun was in his eyes and all he could make out was a female outline dressed in a loose flowing rider's dust coat.

"G'day Frank. I said I might come one day and here I am. I hope you don't mind my turning up like this without warning."

"Jane, the last time you turned up unannounced you managed to save my life. You are always more than welcome to my home. Come here."

He held out his arms to receive her as she glided into his embrace and when he tried to kiss her on the cheek she took his head in both hands and kissed him full on his mouth and made free with her tongue which she knew excited him. Above all this left him in no doubt about her feelings for him.

"Ah Hem!" Coughed Boris. "I am hungry enough to eat a whole steer on my own. Are you two going to postpone the love match and rustle up some breakfast or must I risk the wrath of your cook and go into the kitchen and cook it myself?"

"Boris and Jane. Your arrival is even more welcome than the supply train after the wet and now I will revert to the role of station owner host and extend to you a traditional Kimberley welcome to which all travellers are entitled and especially such dear friends."

For much of the rest of the day they shared their common war experience and caught up on their doings since they had concluded their employment by the government. Jane confirmed that Ibrahim's family was safe because the Australian Ambassador had pointed out how frosty relations might get between Indonesia and Australia if they came to any harm. It was further implied that information about a certain failed special-forces operation could leak out. Also they received Ibrahim's posthumous commendation from the government for his war service and they are receiving a modest but welcome regular pension payment. Frank was pleased to hear this because Ibrahim had proved himself truly to be a man of honour.

Despite Boris's protestations about not seeking station work, frank knew how much he loved this country and before dinner over a couple of glasses of Laphroaig, he invited Boris to join him as a sort of intern starting as a regular stockman with the opportunity to move up to Foreman and most certainly, if Frank was as good a judge of a man as he thought he was, a future manager of a satellite station because he had great expansion plans. Boris proved not to need much convincing.

Frank, Jane, Liza and Dan

After dinner Frank told Jane he had something to show her and that there were people who would want to meet her. He walked arm in arm with her across the yard to the peppercorn trees beneath which the two white gravestones looked exceedingly ghostly in the bright moonlight.

"Liza and Dan. I want you to meet my very special friend Jane about whom I have told you so much. She fought with me in the war and even saved my life. She is not sure about her ability to settle down for long after such a life of movement and action but the Kimberley has infiltrated a corner of her heart and so she is going to give station life a go. What about me? You ask. Well, I think she is more than a little interested in me but she is too wild and independent a woman to commit without much consideration and trial. Ring any bells Liza? But here she is and she can answer for herself."

"Hello Liza and Dan. I have heard so much about both of you and it's a great privilege for me to be invited to work on the station you built up and to team up with Frank who is a very special man- so hard and down to earth on the outside but so subtle and tender within. He lives so many of your values and shares Dan's traits.

In short, he is very dear to me. There, I have said it. He is right that I, and I suspect this is true of him also, do not readily commit and stay at one thing in one place for ever and a day. I am not the conventional marrying kind. But I care for him more than he knows and enough to want to be with him and help him make an even brighter future for the station and its people. So thank you for letting me into your special family and I will strive not to disappoint you."

Frank put his arm around her and wished Liza and Dan, good night.

Through the soft moonlight they strolled arm in arm beneath the branches of the welcoming Boab trees, back towards the house. No word passed between them and they felt no need to talk. The land was doing all the talking tonight and they both knew that whilst no commitment had been made between them. They had made a solemn bargain before Liza and Dan to be good to each other and they would let the Kimberley do the rest.

FOR FREEDOM'S CAUSE

Barry Smith

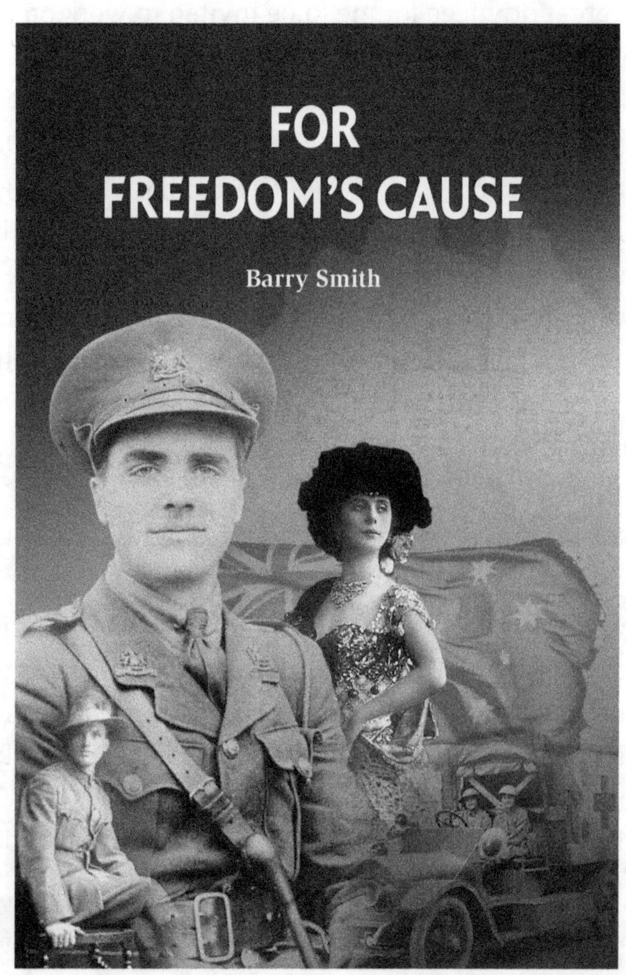

The Kimberley Trilogy
Book 1

FOR FREEDOM'S CAUSE

For Freedom's Cause is the first novel in the Australian dynastic trilogy spanning the First, Second and, yet to come, Third World War. It follows the adventures and growing relationship between a working-class English army officer from Manchester, Dan Bevan, and a Melbourne barrister serving with the Australian Light Horse, Charlie Elliott, who met, by chance during the First World War and the strong women in their lives.

Having survived several major battles, both men are so disillusioned with the homes and occupations they return to, that Dan volunteers to suppress the republican rebellion in Ireland and Charlie joins an underground army to stand-up against mob riots in Melbourne. Despite their contrasting social origins and differing views on what form of government is best for preserving freedom and maintaining civil order, they become firm friends and when Dan is targeted by vengeful IRA assassins, he accepts Charlie's invitation to escape to Australia where he intends settling down peacefully in Melbourne, with the love of his life who unknown to him has borne him a son.

When IRA gunmen pursue him from Melbourne to Perth he is forced to flee to a cattle station in the Kimberley where, finally reunited with his wife and son, he confronts his nemesis in that vast and mystical wilderness.

BATTLE
FOR THE
NORTH
Barry Smith

The Kimberley Trilogy
Book 2

BATTLE FOR THE NORTH

Battle for the North reunites the heroes and heroines of *For Freedom's Cause* – Dan, Charlie, Elspeth Liza and Alice, in frustrating Japanese espionage plots and raids into northern Australia during World War II. The action takes place in the Kimberley wilderness and celebrates the daring and heroism of mounted North Australia Observer Unit patrols, nicknamed the 'Nackeroos' or 'Curtin's Cowboys'.

Following the bombing of Darwin and Broome, Japanese marine commandos land on the Kimberley coast to establish a foothold and deny the US and Australian navies a secure re-fuelling and supply base. With Australia's regular forces deployed in the Middle East and Singapore, all that stands between them and success is Dan Bevan's and Charlie Elliott's part-time observer patrols, which battle a Japanese special forces unit from Broome to their Kalumburu base and join the fight to push the enemy back into the sea.

Flight Captain Daniel Bevan returns from the Battle of Britain to join the air war over northern Australia and whilst Dan and Charlie conduct their guerrilla campaign in the bush, their wives and Lady Elspeth interrupt their war work in Darwin to thwart black market thugs and hunt down a murderous spy.

VICTORIA'S TWINS

I am busy researching background for a book about two of the most significant cities of Queen Victoria's Empire as they emerged from modest beginnings and flourished during the turbulent years of the 19th century.

Gritty Manchester and Marvellous Melbourne experienced the growth in their economies, politics, societies, cultures, infrastructure, media and sport that led to their becoming today's large, influential, internationally famous and vibrant metropolises. As well as one being my birthplace and the other my home, they have much in common and are surprisingly complementary.

Both are home to world famous liberal leaning newspapers and their cities stories are told through the eyes of two of their most illustrious and campaigning editors.

This book will be available in late 2016.

About the Author

BARRY SMITH

Was born in England and educated in Manchester and at Cambridge University, where he read history. Australia has been home for over fifty years and he lives in marvellous Melbourne, where he is now living his dream of being a published writer.

Most of Barry's career has been in HR management and for 20 years before retirement he ran his own consulting business, focusing on turning around toxic management teams. Since retiring he has completed a doctorate focused on *"How I want to live and work in what's left of my life"* and over the past 10 years he has pursued dreams emanating from that – such as, crossing Siberia, touring Moorish Spain, finding his Manchester Regiment, Grandad's grave at Gallipoli, crossing USA by train and camp touring around Australia, carrying out research for and selling his Kimberley Trilogy of historical novels, in pubs and on outdoor markets from Cooktown to Broome and back.

Books about his travels – *Wordspinner's Way*, *My Russian Dreamroad*, *My Spanish Dreamroad* and *My American Dreamrailroad* – recount and illustrate with photographs and 'Brysonesque' commentary, Barry's travels around Australia, selling books in pubs and on markets, living in St Petersburg and crossing Siberia, touring Moorish Andalusia and railroading across the USA from sea to shining sea and back. These can be ordered from Blurb at au.blurb.com.

You can follow Barry's further musings and adventures on Facebook at www.facebook.com/BarrySmithWordSpinner.